A FATHER'S AFFAIR

KAREL VAN LOON is the author of two best-selling novels and a collection of stories based on his travels which was shortlisted for the ECI prize. He has travelled widely as a freelance journalist and television programme-maker. He lives in Amsterdam. *A Father's Affair* has been translated into 16 languages, received rave reviews on first UK publication and sold over a quarter of a million copies in the Netherlands.

SAM GARRETT has worked as a literary translator as well as a freelance journalist. His recent translated works include *The Cave* by Tim Krabbé and *Silent Extras* by Arnon Grunberg.

FURTHER PRAISE FOR
A Father's Affair

"Intriguing, gripping and moving, this novel works on all levels . . . A wholly tragic story with great insight into the heart, love and the workings of human nature. Compelling and compassionate." *What's On in London*

"A Dutch bestseller that brings a thriller-like twist to Dad Lit . . . a story as old as it is universal, but this fresh and funny novel tells it with enough panache to cut through the froth." *Daily Mail*

"Van Loon's novel unwinds with a thriller's pace. As well as tackling the issue of fatherhood, it is also a love story . . . But at its core is an emotive invitation to paranoia, as each stone Armin looks under reveals just how little he knows about the woman he loved – and raises unsettling questions about how much one person can ever know about another." *Observer*

"This is an adult tale, devoid of sentimentality, beautifully crafted, and with courageous honesty and a refreshing lack of self-pity or pretension." *The Herald*

"It was touching, erotic, funny and at times very moving. It raised many questions – how well do we really know those who are closest to us?"
New Books Magazine

"The writing is compelling and careers forward to a disturbing end where death, life and sex come together in one great final revelation." *The List*

"A sort of genetic riddle . . . stunning in its simplicity."
Time Out

"The first half of Karel van Loon's absorbing novel is a beautifully crafted lament for lost love, and a tender paean to a particular kind of parenthood. But the shock revelation about the protagonist's family chromosomes turns *A Father's Affair* into a full-on psychological thriller." *The Times*

"Intriguing, sexy and sad, a beautiful and touching novel."
The Scotsman

"Written in a passionate, charged style. The novel leaps forward as if spring-loaded . . . an exciting, very moving novel written with great talent . . . The writer's overall control is masterly." *De Volkskrant,* Netherlands

"Don't miss this passionate story about love, grief, sex – and the relationship between father and son. The surprising plot makes you want to read it again . . . van Loon is wise, funny, entertaining and profound. If you want to be reminded of what it means to be human, read *A Father's Affair*." *Bergensavisen,* Norway

"A small masterpiece . . . compelling from beginning to end, tense and witty."
Elsevier, Netherlands

"Van Loon applies himself to a classical literary theme and gives it staggering light." *Leipziger Volkseitung,* Germany

"Completely original . . . combines the finest elements of a psychological thriller and literary read." *Elle,* France

A FATHER'S AFFAIR

Karel van Loon

Translated from the Dutch by
Sam Garrett

CANONGATE

First published in English in Great Britain in 2002
by Canongate Books Ltd,
14 High Street, Edinburgh EH1 1TE.
New edition published in 2003.
First published in The Netherlands in 1999 as
De Passievrucht by L. J. Veen.

10 9 8 7 6 5 4 3 2 1

The publishers gratefully acknowledge general
subsidy from the Scottish Arts Council towards
the Canongate International series.

The publishers would like to acknowledge the financial support
of the Foundation for the Production and Translation of Dutch
Literature which helped to make this translation possible.

British Library Cataloguing-in-Publication Data
A catalogue record for this book is available on
request from the British Library

ISBN 1 84195 409 8

Typeset by Palimpsest Book Production Limited,
Polmont, Stirlingshire

Printed and bound by
Cox & Wyman Ltd, Reading, Berkshire

www.canongate.co.uk

For Karin

From the start
Most every heart
That's ever broken
Was because
There was always
A man to blame.

Dolly Parton, 'It Wasn't God Who
Made Honkytonk Angels'

1

We drive to the hospital without a word. Ellen's at the wheel, I'm counting the dots on the macadam. The road is full of cars on the warpath. Ellen drives too fast, then too slowly. She doesn't use her indicators. I say nothing.

Billboards are growing along the side of the road.

THE FUTURE IS HERE.

WHAT MAKES A BUSINESSMAN HAPPY?

'Money,' I say.

'What?'

'No, nothing.'

We park in the concrete belly of the hospital sprawl. Walk down covered streets full of people wearing jogging suits, pushing wheelchairs. On a square, marked by the odour of deep fryers and wilted flowers, a combo is playing gypsy music.

'Left here,' I say.

'There's the lift,' she says.

I look at her reflection in a rectangle of glass. The tension has drained the colour from her lips.

'I don't know how I'm going to take it . . .' she'd said.

'If they say what I'm afraid they're going to . . .'

It's been a few weeks since she completed a sentence.

*　*　*

'Please, take a seat,' the doctor says. And once we're seated: 'I'm afraid I don't have very good news for you.'

I see Ellen stiffen. She tucks her chin to her chest, stares at the floor.

'And especially not for you, sir.'

Her back straightens, her chin pops up. I see it from the corner of my eye. For a second she turns her head in my direction. I'm suddenly aware that I've been sweating heavily; my clothes are sticking to my body, wet and cold.

'You're sterile. And not only is there nothing we can do about it, but – and I realize this will come as something of a shock to you – you always have been.'

The first thing I feel, at least the first feeling I'm aware of when he stops talking, is relief. There must be some gruesome mistake. Files have been switched, test results keyed in wrongly, someone with the same name, sitting in another doctor's office, is being told at this very moment: 'There's absolutely nothing wrong with you, sir. Your sperm is perfectly healthy.'

'But that's impossible,' I say. 'I have a child. I have a thirteen-year-old son!'

For a long time, we sit in silence. Nothing moves. No one moves. The whole hospital sprawl of concrete and steel and glass, the lift shafts, the corridors, the darkened crawlways full of clicking, buzzing, sighing pipes, the rooms full of beds bearing the healing and the dying, the visitors and the physicians, the students and the interns, they all hold their breath. The present holds still, because right behind that present the past is exploding.

Ellen looks at the doctor. The doctor looks at me. I look at a framed photograph right behind his head: a boy and a girl on skis, a snow-lined ridge in the background, a clear blue sky above.

I know that after that things resumed their normal course. That we went on to discuss matters as grown-ups. And that after that we drove home, Ellen and I, down the same roads, past the same billboards, through the same belligerent traffic.

I know, but I don't remember. All I remember is what she asked when we turned into the street where we live.

She asked, 'Do you want to tell Bo?'

Do I want to tell Bo?

There's only one thing I want: that what's been said hasn't been said, that what's happened hasn't happened. It's a senseless thing to want, but there you have it, I can't stop. Stopping would be worse. And so I revise old decisions, go back on what I said before. I reconstruct the recent past in order to preserve an older one. Where I said 'yes', I now say 'no'. Where I had decided to act, I now decide to do nothing. Where I gave in to her desire, because I thought it was my desire, too, there I reject her outright.

'No, I don't want to have a child with you. I already have a child, and that child's enough for me. Let it be enough for you, too.'

I know I'm putting our love on the line, that there will be no future for the two of us if I keep this up, but I do it anyway. Now I do. Because the only thing more difficult than living without a future is living without a past.

2

So Bo was not conceived on a cold summer night in the passenger seat of a yellow Renault 5. He did not get his chin, which protrudes slightly, making it look as if it was put on wrong, from me. His eyes are the colour of Monika's but not the shape of mine, as everyone who knew Monika says. That his left foot is half a size smaller than the right, exactly like mine – pure coincidence.

There's a verse in the Gospel of Philip that I think about often these days. 'The children a woman bears resemble the one she loves. If that is her husband, they resemble her husband. If that is a philanderer, they will resemble that philanderer.'

Once, it must have been about six years ago now, I read that passage out loud to Bo. We were sitting at the wooden table in the kitchen, with big sheets of drawing paper and sharpened pencils in a pyramid of light. I was drawing the House of Knowledge for Bo. First the floor plan, then a front and side view.

'The front room in the House of Knowledge,' I said to Bo, 'is the Room of Factual Knowledge. There you find all the things you know right now. Behind it lies a much bigger room, the Room of the Possible, with all the things you might find out if you live long enough and stay curious.'

Bo rolled a pencil across the tabletop.

Beside the front and back rooms was a space whose outside walls I'd left blank.

'That's God's Dark Room,' I said. 'No one knows how big that room is. Any light you take in there is immediately extinguished. The only way to see anything there is to let your eyes get used to the dark. Then sometimes, just for a moment, you catch a glimpse of things that you would never have thought possible.

'There are people,' I said, 'who are so startled by what they see that they slam the door and never go back in. And there are people who become addicted to it and seldom or never come out again. God's Dark Room is the most wonderful, but also the most dangerous, room in the house.'

The House of Knowledge had a huge attic: the Junk Room of Knowledge, I called it. 'There you find the weirdest things. Funny, useless things, like the Theory of the Flat Earth and the Ten Golden Rules for Debutantes. But also wonderful, useful things, like the Divine Geometry and the Gospel of Philip.'

'What's that about?' Bo asked. And I went to the bookcase and took down the little booklet full of pencilled comments and exclamation marks. I picked out any old passage, completely at random, to read to Bo. It was the passage about the philanderer.

'What's a philanderer?' Bo asked.

'It's someone who loves someone, but only for fun.'

'Isn't it usually fun, then?'

I pretended not to hear. The simplest questions are often the hardest to answer. I drew one final room on the house: a little niche in an empty corner of the floor plan.

'This room doesn't have any windows,' I said. 'It's lit by one bare bulb hanging from the ceiling. It's the room of things you'd have been better off not knowing. I call it the Torture Chamber.'

Bo leaned over the table to get a better look. 'Do you go there sometimes?'

'Yes,' I said, 'I go there sometimes.'

Who is the philanderer Bo resembles? The only person who could tell me that is Monika. Monika died ten years ago.

I could, it occurs to me now, have added another room to the floor plan of the House of Knowledge: the Room of No Hope.

'What do you find in there?' Bo might have asked. And I could have replied, 'Nothing, that's just it. It's a room from a bad dream, a place where you can search all your life for something you know has to be there, but that something keeps slipping away from you just when you think you've found it. It's the room where all the knowledge is stored that you'd like to get to, but for some reason or other can no longer be found.'

Do I want to take Bo to that room?

3

I have a box of pictures from back when Monika was still alive. We'd been planning to paste them up, in three albums with fake black leather covers that she'd bought on Queen's Day. We never got to do it. Later, Ellen used the albums for other photos – pictures of her and me and Bo. Monika's photos are still in that box. For years it lay at the bottom of a cupboard and I never looked at it. But now I've taken it out. From the floor of my study, multiple Monikas are looking at me, five years of my life in Kodak colours on the ground.

Monika in a hotel room on the coast of Brittany. She's three months pregnant, it's morning, dull sunlight is coming through the window. She's wearing a light-blue man's shirt, crumpled, the buttons loose. Her hands are resting on her bare stomach, as if she wants to protect the child. Her white legs dangle over the edge of the high, wrought-iron bed. All through the pregnancy, mornings were hard on her, even after she'd stopped waking up nauseous. In Brittany we walked down to the beach every afternoon, breathed in the sea air to scour our city lungs, watched the seabirds, hunted for shells and starfish among the weedy rocks that fell dry at ebb. One day we found a dead sheep, eaten by fish and birds. The mutilated animal lay there staring at us with empty sockets, like a medieval curse. We hurried back to the hotel.

Monika on the beach at Noordwijk. She's wearing a big red-and-white-striped beach towel, covering her from neck to toes. Her nose is gleaming with suntan oil. Our first summer together. She couldn't stay out in the sun for long. Her red hair turned yellow. Her white skin turned red. Going to Noordwijk had been my idea, on a warm day in July with clear blue skies. Monika agreed to go along, but only because (as she told me later) we hadn't known each other very long and she didn't want to be a killjoy.

'How long can you stay out in the sun?' she'd asked as we were ploughing along through the hot sand, looking for a quiet spot.

'For hours,' I said. 'How about you?'

'Not that long.'

I found her white body enchantingly beautiful, but that day I discovered the price she paid for that beauty. We didn't stay long, and when we weren't in the sea (where we splashed each other, where I took her in my arms in the surf and kissed the salt from her face, where we gave a fervent rendition of the starry-eyed young lovers in a B-movie) – when we weren't in the sea itself she stayed under that big beach towel. Even so, that evening she was sunburned. In the years that followed we often went to the beach together, but never again on a sunny day in July.

There are a few pictures of the two of us. In the most cheerful one, we're riding a big men's bike. Monika's on the saddle, she has to stretch her feet and toes to reach the pedals. I'm sitting on the baggage carrier, one arm around her waist. With my other arm I'm waving at the photographer. I wonder who took that picture, and exactly when it was taken. Judging by Monika's hair, it must have been before Bo was born. After that she let it grow. Just when she'd decided to have it cut short again, she became ill. She was buried with long hair. Now I remember who took the picture: my father. It's my father's bicycle. There are splotches of paint on Monika's trousers. The picture was taken on the Ceintuurbaan, across from the Sarphatipark. We'd just found a house, across the road from the park. My father helped us fix it up.

For the first two weeks, the work left to do increased, rather than decreased, with each passing day. When we scraped off the wallpaper, we discovered that the plaster was crumbling. When we tore out the suspended ceiling, mouldy beams appeared. The chimney had an enormous crack in it. The wooden floor beneath the kitchen cupboards was rotten.

'You should have seen that right away,' my father groused, more at himself than at me. 'What in the world do you look at when you go to see a house?'

'I look out the window, mostly,' I said.

Besides the park, we also had a view of a magpies' nest. The first time I saw the house, the birds were busy repairing their roof. The weather had been wet and blustery, and the large nest had clearly suffered some damage. The two birds were flying back and forth with twigs. It must have been April or May. The picture with the bike was taken two months later. Behind the parked cars you can see a hawthorn in final bloom. Painting the house had been the final chore. Shortly after, we moved in – first Monika, the next day me.

That summer the magpies raised three fledglings. And Monika became pregnant.

4

It was a summer full of firsts. It was the first time I lived with someone. The first time I read the words 'vasopressin' and 'glycogenolysis'. The first time I fucked in a car. The first time I made a woman pregnant (I thought). The first time I ever saw a red-tailed blackbird in Amsterdam (on the Gerard Doustraat). The first time I thought about the words 'It would be foolish to laugh at the romanticist: the romanticist, too, is right' (Ortega y Gasset). The first (and last) time I ever slept with two women at once. The first time I saw my father as my equal, because my father saw an equal in me. That was a change I hadn't seen coming, and one that moved me almost as much as the changes in Monika's body. (Long before her belly began to grow, there were changes in the shape of her face, the pliancy of her hair, the softness of her breasts. I couldn't believe that so many people remained in the dark about it for so long. Did no one really look at her – not even her own mother? No, especially not her own mother.)

My father is a self-made man – those are his own words. He got off to a bad start in life, was weak and sickly as a boy. When he was thirteen, the war broke out. Three months later he lost his father. Not because of the war, but because of a stupid coincidence.

A new house was being built on a street close to where my grandparents lived. The workmen had just installed the highest beam, and my grandfather stopped across the street to see the men congratulate each other, and to watch as one of them, balancing on the tie beam, threw his cap in the air and caught it again. 'If my father hadn't stopped to watch,' my father said, 'that tram would never have hit him.' But, still staring up at the cheering men, my grandfather crossed the street right in front of a number 4 tram. His legs were so badly crushed beneath the steel wheels that they had to be amputated at the hospital. The wound on his left leg (or the stump of it) became infected. The infection became internalized. Ten days after the accident, my father no longer had a father.

'You've never learned to fight,' my father would say whenever he couldn't understand why I did the things I did. What else could I do but admit he was right, and then add as nonchalantly as possible, 'But isn't that exactly what you wanted – to make sure I'd have a better life than you did?'

After the war the family didn't have enough money for my father to continue his education, but he soon found work with a contractor; ironically, the same one who'd built the house that cost my grandfather his life. During the Fifties, when most of Holland was one big building site, my father worked his way up from general dogsbody to foreman. In 1961 he not only married an Amsterdam nightclub singer three years his senior but also started his own business: within ten years, Cornelis Minderhout Contractors & Construction had made my father a prosperous man (even though today's nouveaux riches would laugh at what my father called 'our family fortune' – we had enough money for a duplex in Abcoude and a rowing-boat on the River Gein).

For years I thought of my father as a man who could do anything, an admirable figure who could build a cupola for my attic room as easily as he could whip up a big pan of paella, take apart the engine of our Volvo Amazone or organize a party for a hundred people (to celebrate the fifteenth anniversary of Minderhout Contractors), where a magician performed tricks and my father danced the merengue with a stunning black lady singer. My father is a ladies' man, and although I don't know that he ever cheated on my mother, I can hardly imagine he didn't.

My mother was, as I said, three years older than my father, and when they met she was working nights as a singer ('chansonnière', my father would say) in a club. She was a strikingly beautiful woman, with high cheek-bones and a full mouth that was always accentuated in her publicity photos by dark, shiny lipstick. The wedding pictures clearly show how proud my father was of his conquest. Precisely nine months later, my mother had me. 'Your father was just in the nick of time,' she said later. 'I actually figured I was too old for children.' At the moment of my birth, my father was on a construction site in Leeuwarden. When he came home that evening I was lying in the crib, bathed and powdered. He picked me up, turned to my mother and said smugly, 'Didn't I do a good job on this one?' Years later, when my mother tossed that back in his face, he still had no idea that he'd

said anything wrong. But I was six and sensed unerringly
that my father had hurt my mother, and that made me
keep an even greater distance between us.

'Your father,' my mother said when the time came for
me to leave home, 'has always loved you a great deal.'
But her actually having to say that probably said enough.
(As she lay dying, she said, 'Your father has always loved
me a great deal. But maybe I didn't love him enough. And
later on I couldn't any more.' I didn't dare ask what she
meant.)

But new life changes everything – even, and especially,
the relationship between father and son.

We told my parents that Monika was pregnant on a
lovely, belated summer day in September, a day that
seemed bent on making up for the cold, wet summer
we'd had. They had arrived late in the afternoon, when
the sun was casting a golden-yellow haze over the trees.
The ideal hour for a glass of good wine. (My father
knew everything about wine, too. With great care he
had assembled at the house in Abcoude a wine collection
which, to his considerable pride, had received a write-up
in the local paper. For this special occasion, therefore,
I'd sought the advice of a wine shop on the Frans
Halsstraat, and finally bought a red Bordeaux with a
full bouquet, a touch of oak and an aftertaste with a
slight whiff of vanilla.) The French doors at the front
of the house were open, and the bustle of the street and
the smells from the kitchen, where Monika was fixing
a gorgonzola polenta with three varieties of mushrooms
and a pomegranate sauce, made my parents sigh deeply

over a town in France they'd visited that summer, where they'd dawdled away the hours at pavement cafés with a carafe of full-bodied *vin de pays* and a good book. My father was impressed by my choice of wine. We drank to the good life, and, because I'd brought Monika hers in the kitchen, no one noticed that she was having grape juice rather than Bordeaux.

My father and I took another hard look at the work we'd done that summer (most of it done by Monika and him, because I'd been too busy working – after all, we needed the money), while my mother kept Monika company in the kitchen. When dinner was ready and we were all seated at the table, I said, 'Monika and I have something to tell you.' Then I let a brief silence fall, the way you're supposed to, and looked at my mother, at my father, and back at my mother. My mother smiled benevolently, the way I knew so well, and my father stared pensively at the tablecloth, as if studying a blueprint.

'We're pregnant,' I blurted out, and it sounded clumsy and ridiculous, which it was. You don't tell your parents something as intimate as that, I realized (it's about sex, when you stop to think about it), but by then it was out and, besides, just try stonewalling a pregnancy.

My mother burst into tears. I'd been expecting that. My mother cried readily and plentifully, especially with joy. (She was living proof of how wrong people are when they see crying as a sign of weakness. 'That I won't be around to see how things turn out with you and Bo,' she told me on her deathbed, 'that's what hurts the most.' And she cried then, too. But she died in peace.) But that my father started crying too, that touched me to the quick. He stood up, came over and hugged me. I stood there uneasily, trapped between chair and table, and felt his shoulders shaking. Then he leaned back and looked me straight in the eye. His cheeks were wet, but there was a broad grin on his face. 'From now on, we're no longer father and son,' he said. 'We're both father.' And he went over to Monika and hugged her too, and I hugged my mother and my mother hugged my father and then Monika, and only after that did we dish up the food and fill our glasses. (I went to the kitchen and came back with the carton of grape juice, and everyone laughed at our little ruse.) We talked about everything and nothing, and especially about what it meant to be expecting a child, and I found out that my father had been right: for the first time, we spoke to each other as equals.

When my parents eventually went home, Monika and I waved goodbye from the French doors. Then we sat on the couch, close together, and stared at the candles flickering pleasurably in the belated summer breeze through the open doors, and for a long time we said nothing.

Three days later Monika went to her parents' in Roermond. 'Better if you're not around when I tell them,' she said. And when she came home: 'It's a good thing you weren't around.'

5

First times aren't something you forget easily, but the rest ... My memory's like the filing system of some boozed-up cataloguer: it's full of gaps and improvisations, the drawers have fallen on the floor, the cards have been hastily swept together. Sometimes months go by with no filing activity at all, then the work turns feverish but sloppy. I have a filing cabinet full of memories, but where are the ones that can help me answer the questions that keep me awake these days? Who is the father of my son? With whom did my late beloved betray me? And when? And above all: why? How can it be that I never noticed a thing, that I never had the slightest suspicion? Or is it that the suspicion actually was there, but the drunken filing clerk swept those memories under the carpet, tossed them out the window, incinerated them in the stove?

I look at Bo, who I know better than anyone else in the world, and I see a stranger. I look at Ellen, who I love more than anyone else, and I have to avert my gaze.

Ellen says she wants to marry me.

'Ellen,' I say, 'you want a child. You want a child of your own, and I can't give it to you. Find another man before it's too late.'

'I want to have your child,' Ellen says. 'I don't want

some other man's baby. And I especially don't want
another man. I want you.'

'That's what you say now, but what will it be like in
a year, in two years?'

'How am I supposed to know, Armin? Do you know
what you'll want in two years' time? How do you
know you won't be sick of me? Or that you won't
be in a midlife crisis and run away with a twenty-one-
year-old?'

'Jesus, Ellen.'

'Yeah, Jesus, Armin.'

'But marriage. Why for God's sake do you want to
get married?'

Monika and I never got married. Getting married wasn't
something you did back then. At least, we didn't. We
loved each other, and the State had nothing to do with
something as intimate as love. That went without saying.
And so we didn't marry, not even when the baby came
– in those days, you didn't brush aside your principles
that casually.

We gave Bo his mother's surname (Paradies) – that
went without saying, as well. After all, she'd carried him
for nine months. And she was the one who breastfed him.
That a child automatically received its father's name was
a symptom of the despicable patriarchy under which we
lived. Like Cruise missiles. And capitalism. (The civil
servant at the public registrar's office didn't go along
with our choice of surname. 'That's only possible when
the child isn't officially recognized by the father,' he said.
When I called him a pen-pusher and a lackey, he refused

to deal with our application any more. Finally, one of his female colleagues was called in to settle things – I mutteringly agreed to go along with what the law prescribed. But the next day we placed an announcement in the paper: 'Born: Bo Paradies.' Our parents didn't read *De Volkskrant*. That saved a lot of bellyaching.)

The house on the Ceintuurbaan was really too small for the two of us and the baby. There was no nursery – and everyone knows that a baby has a right to a nursery.

'You two will just have to move,' said Monika's mother, in whom I'd never detected any affection for her daughter, but who felt that she – and no one else – had the right to determine how her daughter's life should be run.

'You could always buy a place,' my father said.

'But Dad,' I said, 'think of all the work we put into this house. And, besides, where else in Amsterdam could you find a house with a view like ours?'

No, Monika and I didn't want to buy a place (you could just see us signing a mortgage with a bank that invested in South Africa!), and we didn't want to move. Bo slept between us in the double bed. We changed his nappies on the couch, on the kitchen table, on the counter, on the floor, on the bed, on the desk between typewriter and telephone. We lugged him around in a sling.

'Like hippies,' said Monika's mother, for whom the Sixties and Seventies had been one long nightmare.

'Like Negroes,' said her father, who thought everyone who hadn't been born in Limburg province was a foreigner, and every Negro a monkey.

'I think it's rather sweet,' my mother said. And my father said, 'If it makes the two of you happy, it'll make the boy happy too. And in the long run, that's what counts.'

And I thought to myself: did he ever say that to my mother about me? But I didn't ask.

The first time Monika breastfed Bo, I sat there crying like a baby.

'It's the hormones,' Monika said.

The next day she asked, 'Do you want a taste?'

I was appalled. But a little later I tasted it anyway. Very cautiously.

'Nice,' I said.

'Liar,' she said.

'It's for babies, anyway, not for grown-up men.'

Monika said, 'It excites me. ' And I asked her, 'Does it excite you when Bo does it?' And Monika nodded.

The last few years I haven't thought much about those days. Only when I see a girl with short red hair, or yellow shoes. Or a man carrying a baby in a sling. But the last few days I haven't thought about much else.

'Give it time,' Ellen said.

'The pain has to wear off,' Ellen said.

'Let's go somewhere for a week, you and me, just the two of us.'

'Go somewhere, you and Bo.'

'Go to Ameland for a week, by yourself, nice long walks along the beach.'

'I want to know who the father is,' I said. 'Who the culprit is. Who's going to tell me that on Ameland? You think his name's written in the sand at the foot of the lighthouse?'

(There's a picture of Monika on the beach on Ameland. In the sand at her feet is written: ARMIN IS CRAZY. She's looking triumphantly into the lens. Her hair is ruffled by the breeze. Our last vacation together.)

'So what do *you* know, Ellen? What do you know that I don't? What did Monika tell you? She must have told you *something*? Girl-talk, don't kid me, I know you talked about those things. Women do that. Who was it, Ellen, come on: who, who, who?'

But Ellen insists that she knows nothing.

'I was in Ecuador then, remember?'

'Yeah, but later, after you got back. She must have said something. Sort of skirted around it, maybe. A little hint, something you didn't pick up on at the time. Jesus, Ellen, the two of you were *intimate* back then. The two of you shared fucking *everything*. And now you're trying to tell me she never said a word about that? Don't lie to me, Ellen. I can't stand any more lies! Oh, Jesus Christ, Ellen, don't start crying. Don't cry, don't cry, don't cry! I'm sorry. I didn't mean it like that, but shit, Ellen, what am I supposed to do? What am I supposed to do with this?'

Later that evening: 'Will you marry me?'

'Yes.'

6

I told Bo that I couldn't have any more children. That my sperm was no good any more.

'Been too long since I used it for what it's meant for.'

That made him laugh. He doesn't mind not having a new little brother or sister. He only thinks it's too bad for Ellen. That's what he said: 'What a drag for Ellen.'

'Yeah,' I said.

And that was that.

When Bo was a baby, I could spend hours looking at him. How he rubbed the sleep from his eyes with fists that weren't fists yet. How he took in the world, without understanding, with those big, hungry eyes. How he burped. How he slobbered. How he discovered the miracle of his own body (those pink things there, right in front of my face, those things belong to me, that's me!).

The day that Bo rolled over all by himself, from his stomach to his back, I bought a bottle of champagne, and that evening Monika and I drank it all. When the bottle was empty, we made love on the floor, against the bathroom door, and finally in bed, doggy style, while Bo lay below Monika, crooning and snatching at her breasts.

'Love, Bo,' I said, when Monika was asleep, 'love, that's what it's all about. The rest is just crap.'

'God is love, Bo,' I said, 'and love is God. There are a lot of misunderstandings about that. Because the first part, a lot of people say that, but the second one, not too many people believe that.'

As long as I kept my eyes open I felt pleasantly drunk, but as soon as I closed them I saw red and yellow spots spinning around like crazy. I burped. Bo laughed. Monika sighed in her sleep. A shadow passed over Bo's face. That brought tears to my eyes.

'Listen carefully, Bo,' I said, 'because this is about the "purification of an 86-kDa nuclear DNA-associated protein complex". And, as you know, you can never start too early on your hard sciences.'

Bo bit his teething ring and looked at me with big eyes.

'"Hela cells,"' I read out loud, '"were cultured in Dulbecco's modified Eagle's medium containing 10 per cent fetal bovine serum." And what do you think happened then? "Gels were stained with a 0.3 per cent Coomassie brilliant blue." It's pure witchcraft, Bo! Modern-day alchemy!'

Just after Bo was born I found work as proof-reader with a scientific publishing house, a job I've held ever since. Every two weeks I picked up a pile of proofs for a professional journal for biochemists, with a worldwide circulation of less than a thousand. At first I struggled with the scientific jargon, but soon I was able to read the articles as easily as recipes in a cookbook, even though the meaning of the recipes remained entirely obscure.

'Who is this mysterious Dr Dulbecco?' I asked Bo. 'And how did that fetal bovine serum end up in this Eagle's medium? What paint shop would you have to go to for Coomassie's brilliant blue? And what do you get when it's diluted to 0.3 per cent – would it turn baby blue?'

Bo threw his teething ring on the floor. I picked it up and gave it back. That was the great thing about correcting proofs: I could do it at home, with Bo around, so I didn't have to miss a single day of his first years of life.

'Go ahead and start working whenever you feel able,' I said to Monika, purely out of self-interest.

'I don't understand how you can collaborate on spreading that kind of research,' she said after she'd spent an evening poring over the journal for biochemists. 'For every article they write, they must kill I don't know how many test animals.'

'That's right,' I said, 'but it pays for the nappies.'

'Oh, sure, hide behind Bo. Burden that poor child with your complicity in the torturing of animals.'

'How do you think they developed the pill?' I asked.

Monika had gone back to work. At Small World, a travel agency specializing in environmentally sound tourism. 'A contradiction in terms,' I said.

'That's right,' Monika said. 'But if you promise not to go on whining about that, I'll keep my mouth shut about the blood of all those innocent animals on your hands.'

And so it went.

Monika started taking the pill again. I divided my attention between Bo's creeping and crowing and 'the temperature dependence of creatine kinase fluxes in the rat heart'.

'"Male Wistar rats,"' I told Bo, who was busy pulling himself up on the coffee table, '"were anaesthetized with diethyl ether and injected intravenously with 50 IU heparin approximately one minute before the hearts were exised." See? Your mother's making a big fuss about nothing. First the anaesthetic, then the heart is removed. How much kinder to animals can you get?'

Bo gave up trying to stand and started crying. With my red pen, I inserted a *c* between the *x* and the *i* in 'exised'.

This morning I woke up at five. I went into Bo's room and sat on the edge of his bed, for at least half an hour. I studied his sleeping features. The shape of his forehead, his hairline, his eyebrows, the colour of his eyes. (Bo sleeps with his eyes open. He didn't always. It started when he was three – with a nightmare.) I examined the little spots in his irises, the length of his lashes, the wrinkles in his eyelids, the slant of his cheekbones, the shape of his nose, the size of his nostrils, the line of his jaw, the shape of his mouth, his lips.

He's entering puberty. There's a pimple on his chin.

I was hoping for a hunch, something in his face that would suddenly remind me of . . . That's what I was hoping for, and it scared me to death.

But nothing happened. Nothing came to me. I crawled back into bed and fell asleep. There was no answer in my dreams either.

7

I'd always thought that Bo was conceived by leave of the Amsterdam police.

Monika and I had been to a benefit performance at the Haarlem Municipal Theatre. A group of famous actors and actresses were putting on a play to help combat starvation in Africa. A few months earlier, the director of the theatre had taken an all-in, four-wheel-drive adventure tour of the Sahara with Small World. Out of gratitude for the care shown, and because he'd made it back alive, he sent complimentary tickets to the travel agency all the time. The play was a crashing bore, but the cocktail party afterwards made up for everything. We identified a large flock of Famous and Prominent People, the salmon was fat and tender, and the wine, the whisky, yes, even the orange juice, were a cut above the average. We stuffed an envelope containing a political statement in the collection box meant for generous contributions ('Starvation is a direct result of the unequal distribution of power in the world. Cancer cannot be cured with aspirin, starvation cannot be stamped out by charity. Support the revolutionary movements in the Third World!'). Then we hung around until long after midnight, observing, drinking, making comments.

When we finally left, an exhausted doorman led us to the stage door, the only door that hadn't already been bolted. Feeling cheerful, we stepped into the chilly June night. Behind us, a famous talk-show host pulled the door closed.

'Let's listen to the nightingales,' I say.

'Nightingales?' Monika asks. 'Are there still nightingales in Holland?'

So I tell her how to drive to the Amsterdamse Bos, where to park the car (in the car park at the start of the old rowing course), and how to walk from there to the nightingales. In the bushes along the shores of the Nieuwe Meer, when we hear the first clear warbles, Monika kisses me solemnly on the forehead. 'Where,' she says, 'do you find a man these days who can lead you straight to a place where the nightingales sing? I'm never going to let you go.'

We sit down on a wet bench that draws the cold right up through the seat of your trousers. I snuggle up close and put my arm around her. My hand lands on her breast.

'We don't do it enough lately,' she says.

'You're right,' I say. 'But we're going to work on that.'

'Hmm, but not here on this bench.'

'No, not on this bench.'

She kisses me. Her lips are dry, but her mouth is warm and moist. She bites my lower lip. The nightingale sings. She puts her hand on my crotch.

'Very good,' she mumbles through the kissing.

My hand slides under her jacket, pulls out her shirt-tails. I kiss her neck, nibble softly on her ear while my hand crawls around her back and slides beneath the edge of her panties. Her buttocks are cold as ice.

'Come on,' I say, helping her to her feet.

'You're horny,' she says. 'I can tell from the way you're breathing.'

'Yes,' I say. I pull her up close and kiss her. 'And so are you.'

'Yes.'

At the car she says: 'Get in. Turn on the heater. And the lights.'

The motor starts with a cough. Monika is standing in the headlights, her face pale, her eyes black. She takes off her clothes. Jacket, shirt, yellow shoes, trousers, panties (she's wearing black underwear; she always wears black underwear when she feels like having sex) – one by one they land on the bonnet. When she's completely naked, she spreads her legs and closes her eyes. She has a pee. The golden stream sparkles in the lights.

'You're crazy,' I say to the inside of the windscreen. 'And glorious. And unbelievably exciting.'

'Turn off the lights,' Monika says, and I obey. In the dark I see the rapid movements of her white body. In the wink of an eye she's beside the car and opening the door.

'Keep the motor running and turn up the heater. My God, it's so cold. And it's almost July! Kiss me, Armin, kiss me!'

She climbs on top of me, pushes her cold breasts in my face. With my left hand, I pull the lever and drop the seat back.

'Take it off,' she says, and slides away from me to put down the back of the passenger seat as well. 'Off, off, off!'

I struggle out of my clothes.

'Sit here.' I slide beneath her onto the passenger seat. My dick is standing crooked as an old tree. Monika grabs my hand and folds it around the trunk. 'Watch,' she pants, 'watch.'

She's crawled onto the driver's seat, her hands glide along her legs, to the dark triangle in her crotch. 'Watch.'

My hand slides frantically up and down.

'Yes!' Monika says. 'That's good. You like that?'

'Yeah.'

'Yeah.'

She leans over, kisses the head of my dick. 'Oh, oh, wait.' She climbs on top of me, and with a hard shove she brings me into her. 'Yes!'

I look at the white of her breasts, I look at the white of her eyes. And suddenly it's as though her whole body is emitting light, Monika has become an angel.

'Shit!' she shrieks. As fast as she climbed on to me, that's how fast she's off me now.

'Shit!'

It feels like something snaps at the base of the stiff organ that has just been generating so much excitement.

'Ow!'

I turn my head and look at the source of the heavenly light. POLICE is written in mirror image between the two round headlights.

'Shihihit,' giggles Monika, in the driver's seat now and

raising the backrest. I lie back down and grab the first piece of clothing I can find. I use it to cover my crotch.

'Jesus!'

I hear a door open. Footsteps. A torch shines into the car. Monika rolls down her window.

'Everything okay, ma'am?'

Monika laughs nervously. 'Yes, everything's okay.'

The light slides slowly over her bare breasts, over my stomach.

'Well then, have a nice evening.'

'Yes, officer, you too.'

More footsteps, the slamming of a car door. From the way the headlights swerve I can tell that the van is reversing, away from us, turning and leaving. Monika leans over, grabs the shirt I was covering myself with, throws it on the floor beside the accelerator and starts kissing my limp cock.

A Renault 5 is awfully small to make love in, but you can. Thirty-eight weeks and three days later, Monika gives birth to a son. We name him 'Bo'.

8

I suffer from Klinefelter's Syndrome, a defect of the sex chromosomes.

'Normally speaking, men have an X and a Y chromosome, while women have two X chromosomes,' the doctor explains patiently when I come back to the hospital for the after-care counselling. 'All egg cells have an X chromosome, while sperm cells have either an X or a Y. When the two cells fuse, it depends on the sperm cell, or on fate, whether you get an XX or an XY: a girl or a boy.'

He uses his silver pen to draw a few neat egg and sperm cells on a piece of paper, and writes the correct letters underneath.

'But what happens with Klinefelter's? Something goes wrong with the formation of the egg cells – an XX cell in the ovary doesn't split neatly into two egg cells with X chromosomes, but splits into one egg cell with two X chromosomes, and one with nothing at all. If the egg cell with the double X is fertilized, you get either a girl with three X chromosomes, which usually has no ramifications whatsoever, or a boy with the chromosomes XXY. The latter is what we call Klinefelter's Syndrome.'

He looks up from his drawing. He's the same man who gave me the bad news a little over a week ago, but it's as though I'm actually seeing him for the first time. He's unusually small, with the limbs of a child, the torso of an old woman, but with the head and features of the lively forty-year-old he seems in fact to be. Ruddy cheeks, greyish-green eyes behind a pair of little gold-rimmed spectacles. He's not unfriendly, but he keeps his distance. I would, too, if I had to explain Klinefelter's Syndrome to a patient.

'The syndrome often leads to clear visible defects,' he lectures on. 'Patients may have an extremely small penis, or they may display slight breast enlargement at puberty. But there are also cases, like yours, in which there are no visible effects at all. Then the presence of the syndrome is discovered only during fertility tests – when it turns out that the semen contains no sperm cells. Unfortunately, that's what one sees in almost all Klinefelter patients.'

SPERM SAMPLES was written in blue letters on the sign above the desk at the IVF clinic. But the cubicle behind the desk was empty. So there I stood, in my hand a brown paper bag containing, ever so discreetly, the little glass jar with my most recent ejaculation. A young couple walked past me down the corridor. I looked at the pharmaceutical company calendar hanging on the blind wall in the little cubicle. The photo on it showed three men in white coats, staring interestedly at the test tube one of them was holding up to the light. The pages of the calendar hadn't been torn off for three months. Maybe someone liked the photo. In one corner of the little office was a doorway opening into a narrow hallway, which led in turn to another room. In that room

I occasionally caught a glimpse of people walking around in hospital uniforms. I tried unsuccessfully to get their attention.

Was there no buzzer? No, there was no buzzer.

Should I shout something? 'Hello, I've got something for you here!'

Behind me I suddenly heard a harsh female voice. 'Just put it down, okay? They'll find it.' I turned around to see who had spoken, but all I saw was the back of a white coat disappearing around a corner.

'Fine, thank you very much,' I mumbled. The sliding window on the desk was half open; it would have been easy just to set my brown paper bag on the counter. But there was something – how shall I put it? – something almost blasphemous about dealing so offhandedly with my sperm. I mean, I rinse it down the drain in the shower every bit as casually if need be, but still . . . that's up to me. When other people start messing around with it, I expect them to show great care, to say nothing of respect – it is, after all, life-giving seed (or so I thought at the time), and despite all medical science still very much a mystery and a miracle and so on. I should have known better. In a hospital, sperm is like urine or foot fungus: something to examine in a lab, something you reduce to a row of digits on a form and then toss in the waste-bin.

I laid the bag on the counter, and just at that moment someone came into the little cubicle. It was the woman who had helped me when I came in, the one who had given me the sticker with my name and outpatient number and date of birth.

When I'd checked in, she'd said, 'Go down that corridor and it's, let's see, the second, no, the third door on
your right, Room C. Any questions?'

Room C consisted of two cubbyholes. One of them
had a toilet and a sink. In the other was a piece of
furniture that looked like a cross between a bed and
an examination table, with a steel frame and black
leatherette upholstery. Next to it was a table with a
huge number of little glass jars. Beside the jars lay stacks
of brown paper bags and, beside those, more stacks of
white towelettes. At the foot of the bed, on a little
rollaway table, were a TV set and a video recorder.

So this was where it was supposed to happen. Solo
sex by the light of fluorescent tubes and a flickering TV
screen.

I read the instructions on the plasticized poster on
one of the immaculate white walls, and did as I was
told. Urinate until the bladder is empty. Wash well
with lukewarm water, but do not use soap. Then I sat
down on the bed and turned on the video. There was an
extreme close-up of a sallow-looking penis sliding over
a shorn labium. I heard excited groans and that typical
smutty-video music. I quickly turned down the sound,
ran the tape back a bit and then cued forward for a long
time. The fuck scene I'd landed in the middle of (and
during which my predecessor had reached his climax?)
was followed by an outdoor scene. A pale man with a
typical Seventies look (hair down over his ears and a
flimsy smile on his face) was leading an equally pale
woman down into the cabin of his houseboat. The next
moment she was on her knees, giving him a blow job. A

second man came on board and did what men in porno films always do. Suddenly the camera was panning after a young woman on a bicycle. Her blonde pigtails flapped in the wind. She stopped at a farm, dumped her bike against the wall of an outbuilding and, bingo, there she was rolling in the hay with a lusty hired hand who hadn't even bothered to take off his gumboots.

It was no mean trick to find a sequence that could, by any stretch of the imagination, be called exciting, but eventually I stopped the video at a badly focused breast in backlight. There was also, I had to admit, something exciting about masturbating in an almost-public space. Besides that, the porno movie was ridiculous, and humour is the ideal accompaniment to lust. Hence the deadly earnest of fundamentalist preachers. I took a little jar from the table, stood beside the bed, took another good look at the breast on the screen, closed my eyes and thought the kind of thoughts that can bring you to a sexual climax. (Contrary to what the books of feminist heavyweights like Nancy Friday and Shere Hite would have us believe, most people – if they fantasize at all – fantasize not about wild orgies, panting Great Danes, or bondage, but simply about their own partner, or about partners from the past. To that rule I am no exception.)

It was a little hard to keep the jar at the right angle at the right moment, but it all worked out without any mess. As I pasted on the label, I had to laugh out loud. If it hadn't been for having to cross the waiting room where two lonely men were emphatically engrossed in an old back-issue of a magazine, while a

prim couple – who I judged at a glance to be of the
we-decided-late-because-our-careers-came-first school –
were poring over the birth announcements on the giant
bulletin board – if I hadn't had to walk through there,
I'm sure I would have sung or whistled a tune, that's how
cheerful this uncommon ejaculation had made me.

But the wait at the SPERM SAMPLES desk soon turned
my cheerfulness back into the initial nervous embarrass-
ment. Eye to eye again with the woman who had done
my intake, I wondered how many minutes had passed
and whether I hadn't come much too fast, or actually
taken a perturbingly long time. I laughed awkwardly
and said, 'Here you are.' And she said, 'Thank you very
much.' And that was that.

The doctor makes another attempt at helping me put
things in perspective.

'You are not,' he says, reinserting his pen in the breast
pocket of his white lab coat, 'the only man made sterile
by Klinefelter's Syndrome who has nevertheless raised a
child. A study in England among twelve married patients
showed that three of them had a child. One man even had
a number of children. Whether those men's wives were
still alive to explain things, of course, I don't know.'

That last sentence he mumbles under his breath, as
though suddenly realizing that this titbit of information
will do little to help me come to terms with the insane
truth that my son is not my son. And that the woman
responsible for that fact is no longer around. (Fate had
had another cruel twist in store. The fertility test was
originally carried out because Ellen, after two years of

trying to get pregnant, was wild with desperation – a desperation I understood, but didn't share. The first time we went to the hospital, they asked us about any congenital defects in our families. 'Two uncles and my grandfather on my mother's side,' Ellen said, 'went mad and spent their lives in an institution. I remember my one uncle sitting in a chair, drooling like a helpless baby, and asking over and over again: "Where are the jujubes? Has anyone seen my jujubes? Who took the jujubes?"' 'There's a slight chance,' the doctor said, 'that you carry a gene which increases the likelihood of insanity. So, just to be on the safe side, we'll run a chromosome test.' The result of that test was maddeningly comforting: if we'd been able to have a child, that child would have had just as much or just as little chance of going insane as anyone else.)

'Fate,' I say to the photograph of the two happy teenagers in powder snow above the doctor's head, 'is crueller than the cruellest butcher in a concentration camp.'

'There is no sense in ascribing human characteristics to fate,' he finds. 'Fate is blind – all natural laws are blind.'

'What makes you so sure of that?'

'Well, that's been my experience. I've never been able to discover any justice in the way one person is struck by disaster and illness and the other isn't. Have you?'

'I wasn't talking about justice, I was talking about cruelty.'

'Those are,' he says, 'two sides of the same coin. Without a sense of justice, there can be no cruelty.'

'Of course, but the absence of justice you've noted says nothing at all about the nature of fate, does it? Does that rule out fate being cruel? When you simply observe the actions of the butcher in the concentration camp, you have no idea whether he has any sense of justice – and therefore no idea whether he's acting out of cruelty or out of complete stupidity.'

'Well, all right,' the doctor concedes (there's probably another patient waiting), 'we're all free to think about these matters as we please.'

But I'm in no mood to be put off with platitudes. Not now. Not under these circumstances.

'No, we're not all free to do that!' I shout. 'First you say that I shouldn't ascribe human characteristics to fate. Then I show you that you know nothing, *nada*, about the character of fate – human or inhuman, cruel or stupid: you simply don't know, and then you try to get out of it with some gobbledygook!'

I've jumped to my feet and I'm screaming at him like a fishwife – and it feels wonderful.

'No, that's not what I . . .' he mumbles.

'Precisely! There you go! That's not what you meant! But what *did* you mean? I know your type, I know exactly what you mean. Day in, day out, I do nothing but read meaningless studies by all those colleagues of yours, big, impressive-looking stories about calcium-ionophores and endothelial cells and shit like that! Advanced motor mechanics, that's all it is. How substance A interacts with substance B, and what that means in turn for the permeability of membrane X. And because you guys happen to be smart enough to unravel a few of those extraordinarily complicated problems – resulting, by the way, in a whole slew of new and even more complicated problems – out of pure euphoria at that success, you now think you can explain the whole fucking universe. God is dead! Fate is blind! Everything is random! Everything is senseless, irrational, out of control! But as soon as anyone bothers to ask you to defend those standpoints by force of argument, you guys pretend there's no one home. Then suddenly everyone is free to think whatever they want. God, what intellectual cowardice!'

I suddenly realize that I'm shaking all over. The room has gone liquid, the doctor is swimming, office chair and all, to the window and back.

'Oh, fuck,' I moan, falling back in my chair. I crumple into a ball. Bury my face in my hands. I feel the salt of tears stinging my eyes, but I refuse to start crying now.

'Oh, fuck,' I say again, and run away as fast as my rubber legs will take me. 'Mr Minderhout!' I hear the stunned doctor's assistant call after me. 'Mr Minderhout!'

The hospital is conspiring against me. Corridors blend into other corridors without getting me where I want to be. Signs point me in the wrong direction. Lifts take me to the wrong floors. I bump into rolling trolleys. Trip over a child, which begins crying loudly. Its mother curses me up and down.

I duck into a stairwell where the stairs all lead upwards. I run, jump, three steps at a time, going up. I climb and climb until I reach the highest floor, completely out of breath. There's another corridor. At

the end of it, daylight is rushing in. I stumble towards it.
There's a sofa beside a coffee table covered in magazines.
I fall onto the sofa. The blood is pounding at my temples.
My back is soaked with sweat.

'Are you all right?' a woman's voice asks.

When I look up again, I'm lying, fully dressed, on a
hospital bed beside a window. I have a broad view of
a park, fields, a motorway. In the distance I see two
steeples. Abcoude. And I think about my father and
suddenly I know for sure that I'll never tell him what's
wrong with me. It would make me feel as inferior as I
did when I was a boy and cringed every time he said,
'Isn't it about time you started going after girls, instead
of watching birds?'

'Sure, Dad.'

A kestrel is hanging in the wind like a kite.

'A cup of tea will do you some good,' the woman's
voice says.

I turn my head and look at her. YASMIN AL-MUTAWA
is printed on the little name-tag on her breast.

'Thank you, Yasmin,' I say, but my mouth is so dry
and my voice so quiet that I can't even hear myself.

9

Last night I went out drinking with Dees, for the first time in seven months. After the second glass of whisky I told him what had happened.

'My God,' Dees said. 'Waiter, could we have two more? Better make that doubles.'

Dees is a scientific editor. We work for the same publisher. I've known him for thirteen years. He's my best friend. He knew Monika, too.

'My God, Armin, who would have expected that from Monika?'

'Yeah.'

'Jesus! And I always thought Bo looked so much like you.'

We sit and say nothing and drink our double whiskies.

'Do you have any idea,' Dees asks, 'who it could have been?'

'No. You? For starters.' We both burst out laughing.

'No. Someone at that travel agency where she worked?'

'Could be.'

'Wasn't there some ex-boyfriend, a guy she still saw sometimes?'

'Yeah. Robbert.'

'Jesus, man!'

'Yeah.'

'Have you told Bo?'

'No. Only that I can't have any more children.'

'Probably just as well.'

'I don't know.'

There's a television above the bar. A blonde is lying on a bed. Candles are burning. She has the sheet pulled up just over her breasts.

'You have to go now,' the subtitle reads.

A man runs his hand through his hair. He stands at the bedroom door, takes a step towards the bed, changes his mind, turns around and leaves. The woman starts weeping. In close-up, you can see her mascara running.

'Remember that time the four of us went to the beach?' Dees asks. 'When Bo was still a baby?'

I nod.

'He was on your back, in one of those slings. And you were gabbing away at him as if he was fifteen, instead of eight months old. Picking up shells and pieces of driftwood and showing them to him. Monika and I stood there and watched you walk along the waterline. What you didn't know was that Bo had been asleep for a long time.'

He takes a sip of whisky, looks up at the TV screen, stares into his glass. He looks tired. Dees always looks tired. For as long as I've known him, he's led the life of a dyed-in-the-wool bachelor. Works too much. Eats badly. Drinks a lot. Sleeps too little. Bachelors are more faithful friends than attached men are. I'm living proof of that: since Ellen and I have been together, Dees has seen a lot less of me. But complaining would be as foreign to Dees as clean living.

He says, 'Then suddenly I notice that Monika's crying. I can't take it when women cry. It makes me nervous as hell. She grabs my hand. I want to put my arm around her, but it doesn't work. You're running down the beach with Bo on your back and you don't have a clue. And I wait until Monika's finished crying. She lets go of my hand. Pulls out a handkerchief and wipes her face. I wanted to ask what she was crying about, but I couldn't find the words. Women crying. I've never been able to handle that.'

'Yeah,' I say. We order two more whiskies and two beers.

'All this talking makes a body thirsty,' Dees says.

'Men!' Monika would have said. 'They drive me nuts!'

Later that evening, after we've said all there is to say about the condition of the playing field at the Amsterdam Arena, long after the weepy blonde has thrown herself from the roof because the man at the door left her again, and after the barman has switched to Elvis, Dees suddenly says: 'Of course, it *is* a perfect case example for the old nature *v.* nurture debate.'

'What, the grass in the Amsterdam Arena, or that woman's suicide?'

'No, the business with Bo.'

'Oh, that.'

'Yeah. I mean, Bo looks so much like you, but he doesn't have your genes.'

'Oh. Yes. I guess I never looked at it that way.'

I'd planned to run through a pile of proofs this morning,
but I get out the box of photos instead. There's one of
Monika and Robbert. It was taken at a party at our
house on the Ceintuurbaan. They're holding up their
glasses in a toast. Robbert is grinning at the camera.
Monika is smiling her Monika smile: restrained, but
with that cynical little something. (There were people
who hated her for that smile, but those people couldn't
see the pain behind it.)

Could he be the one? Robbert? No, couldn't be.
Couldn't it be? Bo doesn't look like him at all. Well,
except for the colour of his hair. Where might Robbert
be these days? What would a law-school dropout be
doing for a living? Running a consultancy? Doing a little
day-trading? Would he still be living in Amsterdam? I
haven't seen him for years. I pick up the phone book.
Haakman, Humadi, Huisman, Hueber.

Hubeek, H.J.M., attorney – impossible.

Hubeek, R.P.F. – damn, that's right. 'The Reformed
Political Federation called for you,' I used to say to
Monika whenever I'd had Robbert on the line. 'Is
Monika there?' were the only words he ever spoke.
He never asked how I was doing, or about Bo, but
that seemed only logical to me. He didn't like me, and
the feeling was mutual. On the few occasions Monika
went out with him while we were together, she came back
with stories about how narrow-minded he was, what an
enormous stick-in-the-mud. He came to our house only
once, for that party. We shook hands. He wasn't at the

funeral. I can't remember whether he received a funeral announcement.

Hubeek, R.P.F. I jot down the address and telephone number in the back of my pocket diary. From the looks of things, he's gone up-market.

'Do you think it could have been somebody at Small World?' I ask Ellen that evening.

'Of course not.'

'What do you mean, "Of course not?"'

'You tell me what kind of men worked there.'

'I don't know.'

'You had Chris Verhoeven. He was a fag. Then you had Chris Winters. He wasn't Monika's type at all.'

'Why not?'

'The kind who wears slip-on trainers and trousers with an elastic waistband. A single family dwelling in Almere with no family.'

'And who else?'

'Who else? Well . . . well, there was Niko.'

'Exactly.' I remembered Niko. The tour guide. Pale face. Straight, dark hair. Dark eyes. A little tatty. The kind of guy who made other men wonder why so many women fell for him. Couples who booked a tour with Small World in order to save their relationship were better off not ending up in Niko's group.

'Niko's destroyed a lot of marriages,' Monika said when she introduced me to him at an office party. (The same party where I first met Ellen. 'This is Ellen,' Monika said. 'If I ever leave you for anyone, it'll be for her.')

'Impossible,' Ellen says. 'I would have noticed. I had a crush on him myself back then, remember?'

'That's exactly it. It would explain why she didn't tell you.'

'Armin, Armin, stop it. You're driving yourself crazy.'

'No I'm not. I'm doing everything I can to stop myself going crazy.'

I've written Niko's name in the back of my pocket diary, too. Under Robbert's. Ellen has no idea where Niko lives these days, or what he does. But I'll find out: Neerinckx, written with a ckx at the end. There can't be too many of those in Holland.

10

The first words a child learns are, I believe, the most important ones in his life.

It's better for a kid to learn 'monkey', 'nut', 'kitten', 'fire' and 'peanut butter sandwich' than it is 'Atari', 'Nintendo', 'Teletubby' or 'My First Sony'. Better yet if he learns 'sparrow', 'titmouse', 'blackbird', 'magpie', 'redwing'. Or 'love', 'is', 'as', 'wine', 'and', 'balsam,' 'all', 'who', 'anoint', 'themselves', 'with', 'it', 'revel', 'therein'.

Bo's standing at the edge of the pond, throwing bread crusts at the ducks. He's making a lot of noise while he's at it. Especially when the seagulls dive into the ruckus on the water.

'Seagull!' he shouts then. 'Seagull, pretty!'

Bo is wild about gulls. We have a standard Sunday-morning ritual: the gull-feeding ritual. We go out on the balcony together, at the back of the house. All week we've been saving heels of bread. 'Seagull!' Bo shouts. 'Seagull, pretty!' And as soon as the first black-headed gull comes sailing over the rooftops, he throws a crust into the air as hard as he can. Following a brief little trajectory, that first crust always lands in the downstairs neighbours' garden, but seldom does that escape the gull's eye. Within minutes the air is filled with shrieks that quickly drown out Bo's shouting. The high point is always that moment when, with an unerring dive, a gull succeeds in intercepting an earthbound piece of bread. Then the two of us cheer and clap till our hands hurt. The wild pursuit (by jealous gulls who have just missed three times in a row) that follows such a tour de force receives our undivided attention.

'Jealousy,' I tell Bo, 'is a very healthy emotion. As long as it's accompanied by intense physical effort.'

Bo can nod so sagely.

Bo likes ducks, too, but he clearly likes them less than gulls. In the pond is a drake with a crippled wing. The wing dangles in the water like an afterthought. Bo thinks the handicapped drake has more right to a crust of bread than the others. But, no matter how he tries, the poor bird never catches a crust. The healthy members of his own sort, or the gulls, are always too quick for him. For the first time, Bo is not pleased with the gulls' aerial skill.

'Go 'way,' he shouts. 'Go 'way!' But the gulls won't be put off by a toddler. 'Stupid gulls,' he mutters. And, a little later on, 'Stupid duck.'

It's a small step from pity to disdain. A step even a child of two years and three months can take with ease.

'There are two trees growing in Paradise,' writes the apostle Philip. 'The one brings forth beasts, the other men. Adam ate of the tree that brought forth beasts. And he became a beast and brought forth beasts.'

11

Bo has gone to bed. The TV is off. I'm trying to read a book about the extinction of species, written by an island biogeographer (that seems like an extremely attractive profession of late: island biogeographer), but I can't concentrate. Ellen comes out of the kitchen with two glasses of wine. I put down the book.

'What's your fondest memory of Monika?' she asks when we've touched glasses and tasted the wine.

'The first evening the three of us were together,' I say without hesitation.

'Really?'

'Really.'

'Or are you just saying that to make me feel good?'

'Does it make you feel good?'

'Yes.'

'Good. But that's not why I said it. No one could share the way Monika did.'

'How do you remember that evening?'

Like this.

No one started it. Suddenly there were three mouths coming together, three tongues exploring. Ellen's face was still wet with tears. Monika had breadcrumbs in

her hair. A tram rumbling down the Ceintuurbaan was
making the house shake. We kissed each other with all
the tenderness we had in us, with all the desire for love
and attention and affection of young adults. We kissed
each other out of curiosity.

And like this.

Monika's hands were covered in breadcrumbs. On the
counter, a sea bass on its platter was staring at the blue
tiles of the kitchen wall. The fish was surrounded by
bottles and jars of herbs and oil, capers and olives. There
was an open bottle of cognac and a bag of macaroons.
Next to that a plastic sack full of peaches. There was
a dish of exotic-looking vegetables. On the baking tray
were fresh sardines. The baking tray was resting, for
lack of a better place, on top of the fridge.

'Tuscan kitchens are bigger,' Monika said ruefully.

'Can I help?'

'No.'

The table in the front room had already been set, for
three. Beside each plate was a card of hand-made paper
on which Monika had written the menu in a graceful
hand. The hors d'oeuvres consisted of crostini with mus-
sels and *sarde alla griglia*. After that the menu promised
spaghetti with olive oil and garlic, followed by *branzino
aromatizzato al forno*. By way of vegetables we'd be
having *finocchio gratinato*. The dessert was a Tuscan
surprise, *pesche con amaretti*. (I found one of the menu
cards when I was looking through the box of photos. It
had a stain on it. A tear, I thought sentimentally.)

'Red or white?' I shouted to the kitchen.

'Red first, then white with the fish. And I bought a dessert wine.'

'You must love us very much.'

'Either that or I have a drink problem.'

Ellen arrived with windblown hair, looking flushed. 'Headwind,' she apologized.

Monika hugged her. 'It's so *good* to see you again. God, you look good! Don't you want to put on something dry? You're all sweaty. Come on, I've got something for you.' I went to the kitchen to uncork the wine.

Maybe you could say that that's how it started: with Monika dressing Ellen up in her own clothes. They must have stood in front of the floor-length mirror together and tried out one outfit after the other – later on, the bed was covered in clothes. They were giggling and shrieking.

'Be there in a minute, okay?' (Ellen.)

'Pour us a glass of wine!' (Monika.)

I watched the three young magpies chasing each other around the crown of the chestnut. The tree was shaking in the wind. The house filled with mirth.

'Look,' Monika said. 'Isn't she beautiful?'

Ellen did a little pirouette. She *was* beautiful. She was wearing a short, sleeveless, off-white dress, a birthday present from Monika's mother. 'Just like my mother to give me a dress that makes me look pale and skinny,' Monika had grumbled. She'd never worn the thing.

Ellen had a deep tan; her dark hair made her look a lot more like a woman named Monika than Monika did.

'Keep it. God, aren't you beautiful. Isn't she, Armin?'
'Yeah.'
I handed them their glasses.
'To a wonderful evening.' (Ellen.)
'To a safe homecoming.' (Monika.)
'To us.'
'So how was Ecuador?'
That was the question that made Ellen cry.

This is the Ecuador she took us to that evening. High mountains with eternal snow at the summits. Thin air. Stony soil that barely supports life. Indians in woollen ponchos and black hats. The Holy Virgin weeping on every street corner. Change as slow as the wearing away of rock by the wind.

'So one day we went to the market in Otavalo,' Ellen said. 'It's the most famous market in South America. You can buy really great Indian stuff there: clothes and baskets, jewellery made of glass and gold. We got into town early in the morning on the bus from Quito, and by noon there was no doubt about it: the market in Otavalo was going to be part of our Ecuador programme.' ('We' was Ellen and her colleague Niko Neerinckx, whom she had a crush on but who left her love unrequited – though we only heard about that much later in the evening, when things like that no longer seemed like intimacies, just things you shared without thinking.)

'Niko bought a few souvenirs,' Ellen told us, 'and wanted to go back to the hotel to work on his notes and write a few postcards. I decided to go to the monastery of San Francisco, which is this big colonial building in the centre of Quito. In front of the statue of Jodocus Rijke, the founder of the monastery, there was a woman begging. She had a little boy with her, about ten years old, with these big empty eyes. I gave her some change, and we started talking. She said she needed the money for her sister, who was in the *cárcel de mujeres*, the women's prison, on the north side of town. I asked why her sister was in jail. For dealing drugs, she said. She'd been in there for three years, and she still had seven years to go. The whole time she was talking, that little boy just sat there staring at me. This is her son, the woman said. He hasn't spoken a word since his mother went to prison. If I wanted to, the woman said, I could go with her at the end of the afternoon to visit her sister. She'd like it if an *extranjera* came to visit. I said I'd go, and I promised to meet her back at the statue after I'd visited the churches and chapels inside the monastery. "Say a prayer for my sister," the woman said. "Her name is Felicia."'

Ellen took a sip of wine and stared at the wall. When she started talking again, her voice sounded different. More fragile. 'In the chapel of Señor Jesús del Grande Poder,' she said, 'I lit a candle for Felicia. And later I went and visited her in the *cárcel*, with her sister and the little boy who didn't say anything. It was so . . . It was so horrible.'

She started crying without making a sound. Monika moved over beside her and put an arm around her.

'That woman was a living corpse. At night the rats had bitten her feet and the wounds were . . . The smell, I'll never forget it . . . And that poor boy, he just sat there.

The way he looked at his mother! And she didn't want to see him. She avoided looking at him.'

Ellen pressed her face against Monika's breast.

'Oh, girlie,' Monika said, 'girlie, girlie.' And Ellen cried and Monika kissed her hair and signalled to me with her eyes. I sat down on the other side and put my arms around both of them, and Monika said: 'That's better.' And Ellen looked up and smiled through her tears.

We kissed until the tears dried up. Then we sat down at the table. That's how it started.

'Yes,' Ellen says. 'That's how it started.'

It's as if we've walked into a room together and the door has swung shut behind us. We sit beside each other on the couch, still as can be. We're listening to the ticking of the clock. The clock is ticking away the seconds of fourteen years ago.

Under the table our feet continued the exploration. Across the table our eyes and lips told different tales. Monika was relating the latest gossip from The Small World. I said something about biotechnology and the *Escherichia coli* bacterium. Monika said I was spoiling her appetite, and changed the subject by asking Ellen about Andean cuisine. As it turned out, that spoiled her appetite, too. (The most popular dishes in Ecuador are *yaguarlocro*, soup with pieces of blood sausage, and *cuy*, roast guinea pig.)

We ate and drank and otherwise spoke of nothing. We drank the dessert wine on the floor, Monika and I leaning against the couch, Ellen across from us. Monika laid her legs across Ellen's knees. Ellen laid a hand on my leg. I laid my head on Monika's shoulder. Candles glowed, the wind brought rain, it was early August but the evening smelled of autumn.

When the dessert wine was finished, Monika asked Ellen: 'Do you want to sleep here?'

'Yeah, that's a good idea,' she said.

I opened another bottle of red and put on a record. Joan Armatrading sang, 'It could have been better', but it couldn't have been.

'You can,' Monika said when the wine was finished and the only thing that broke the silence was the sound of a tram on its way to the terminus, 'sleep on the couch. But you can also sleep in our bed.'

Ellen looked at me. 'Sure,' I said.

'Okay, that's good,' Ellen said.

'I knew right then what was going to happen,' Ellen says.

'Really?'

'Yeah. Didn't you?'

'No . . . I didn't have a clue.'

'Then you didn't know Monika very well.' It's out before she realizes it. She quickly lays her hand on my leg. 'I'm sorry, I didn't mean it that way.' But I'm not letting myself be yanked out of the past, I'm not going to let in the pain of right now, not now that I'm wallowing in the innocence of back then.

'How did it happen?' I ask. 'How do you remember it?'

'Monika said that the two of you always slept in the

nude, but that you could put something on if I felt
better about that. And I said no, you don't have to. I
like sleeping naked, too.'

'No one asked me a thing,' I say.

'No,' Ellen says. 'It was Monika's party. The whole
evening was Monika's party.'

'You're right.'

Never have I met anyone who could be so command-
ing, but who made sure at the same time that nothing
happened you didn't want to happen. (Although what
you *did* want didn't always happen, because you didn't
get around to deciding for yourself what that was. Much
later, I realized that had occasionally made me feel left
out, but by then Monika had been dead for a long time.
And her death made me feel left out a lot more. Her death
made all her faults completely irrelevant – all except one,
I know now. But I push away that thought, too.) I say, 'I
liked the way your breasts were so white, compared to
the rest of your body.'

'And your skin was softer than I'd expected a man's
to be. And Monika was so beautifully white, almost
translucent.'

'Yeah. Almost translucent,' I say. And then, 'I guess
she's the one who started.'

'No,' Ellen says. 'It was me.'

'You? Really?'

'Yeah. I was lying in the middle. I could stroke your
legs and her . . .'

'Her what?'

'Her . . . uh . . .'

'Is that how it started?'

'Yeah. My hand landed right on her . . . uh . . . her pubes. I could tell she liked that. And I could tell you liked it when I touched your leg.'

'You know,' I say, 'before that night I'd never been to bed with anyone except Monika.'

'No! You're kidding! Really? Jesus, that's so sweet.'

'Wasn't Monika the one who said I should lie in the middle?'

'Yeah. It was her party the whole time. And maybe she felt a bit threatened, with her best girlfriend lying there beside her boyfriend, naked in bed.'

'That's right,' I say, 'she told me that later on. That she was afraid I'd fall in love with you. She was in love with you, but she said that was different. I didn't find it threatening. Weird, huh?'

'Monika got excited by looking at how I touched you,' Ellen says.

'She always got excited when I touched myself,' I say.

'Really? Oh, I don't have that at all.'

'No, I know.' We both laugh about that. It's a laugh of relief. I top up our glasses. But the door is still locked, we're still caught in the events of fourteen years ago.

'I thought her kisses were really exciting. She moved her tongue really slowly, but really – how can I put it? – determinedly.'

'It excited me to watch you two kiss,' I say. 'I'd never seen Monika kiss anyone else. Fortunately.' And once again I push away all thoughts of the present. I want to think the way I thought then, feel what I felt then.

'Monika asked whether I wanted to see how you two did it,' Ellen said.

'Yeah, that intimidated me a bit.'

'But it was Monika's party, so . . .'

'Yeah.'

'I liked the way you did it. So carefully.'

'That was partly because you were there. We didn't always do it that carefully, of course.'

'I liked it that you two didn't want to come.'

'Yeah, that would have been shutting you out.'

'Yeah.'

'But you didn't come then, either, did you?'

Ellen doesn't say anything. Takes another sip of wine.

'What? You mean you . . . No, really?'

Ellen almost chokes on her wine. 'Oh yeaaah!' she cackles. 'Oh-yes-indeed-I-did! But then I'd been lusting around for a month in Ecuador, remember? Longing for that terribly attractive but oh-so-unreachable Niko. And when I saw the two of you going like that . . . Jesus, Armin, I'm sorry, but I had to think about Niko, and then . . .'

'So that's why you started going on about him.'

'Yeah. That's why.'

'I thought that was so sweet.'

'Really?'

'Yeah.'

When Ellen told us about her unrequited love, Monika had said, 'I have something to tell you guys, too.'

That little smile was playing at the edges of her lips again, the smile that enraged other people, but which I loved every bit as much as her brazenness.

'I'm pregnant,' Monika said.

Ellen and I looked at her, looked at each other.

'I'm two weeks late,' Monika said. 'This morning I did one of those tests. I'm expecting.'

'Jesus, Monika! Really?'

'Yeah, really!'

'But why didn't you say?'

'This is a much better moment, isn't it?'

'My God!'

'Congratulations.'

'Thank you.'

'Oh! Oh wooow!'

'Where's the wine? We must drink to this!' But the wine was finished and Monika said she wasn't going to drink another drop for the next seven and a half months.

We laid our heads on Monika's stomach, first me, then Ellen. We listened and spoke quiet words. I kissed her cunt. Her cute, girlish cunt.

'Yeah,' Ellen says. 'She had a cute, girlish cunt.'

The door opens. It's Bo. 'I can't sleep,' he says.

'Do you want a glass of wine?' Ellen asks. (It's gone so fast, I think. Bo drinking wine!)

'Yuh,' Bo says. He's wearing an oversized T-shirt ('I'm Bart Simpson. Who the hell are you?') and sweat pants. He sits down in an easy chair and folds his legs under him. He's getting tall. He's definitely going to be taller than I am. He takes a sip of wine.

'Not bad,' he says. And then, 'Is this a bad moment?'

'No, Bo, this isn't a bad moment.'

12

Children and cars have one thing in common: women don't love them any more or any less than men do, just differently. Monika got angry at Bo more often than I did, but she also forgave him more easily. And if I manoeuvred her into a situation where she had to choose between him and me, she always chose him, without question. (Upon which I would sit in a corner and mope demonstratively, as if not Bo but I were the child that needed her unconditional love – and maybe that was right.)

Monika was also deeply in love with her canary-yellow Renault 5, in which she had escaped her suffocating youth in Roermond. That I one day wrote that car off in a collision with a brand spanking new BMW 524 Turbo Diesel was pure coincidence, however, and had nothing to do with jealousy.

I'd taken Bo to the woods at Spanderswoud, where we'd spent the day in the company of mushrooms, bracket fungi, leprechauns, dung beetles and spider webs. How we'd hit on it I can't remember, but by the time we were driving back into Amsterdam talk had turned to love. I said, 'Love is what makes life. Without love, everything dies. That's been scientifically proven.'

Bo was sitting in the back, safely strapped into his car-seat. He was probably watching the traffic tear by, or playing with a chestnut. I wouldn't even rule out the possibility that he was asleep: our little talks sometimes took the form of long, uninterrupted monologues on my part ('a lot of hot air', Monika called them).

'A hideous experiment was once performed on baby monkeys,' I told him. 'Some of the monkeys were taken away from their mothers at birth and put in a bare cage, with nothing but a bottle and a nipple they could drink from. Other monkeys were put in the same kind of cage, but were given a doll wrapped in a piece of soft fur: a sort of artificial mother. The third group of monkeys were allowed to stay with their mothers. And what do you think happened? The monkeys in the bare cage without a doll drank the milk and spent the rest of the time in a corner, shivering in terror. The monkeys with the doll clamped onto it – so tightly they wouldn't even let go long enough to drink. They preferred starvation to leaving their artificial mother. Later on, studies were made of how the different groups had developed. The ones who'd been in the bare cage were the worst off. They couldn't deal with other monkeys, and they were the first ones to go down with diseases. The monkeys who had been given a doll caught up in physical development after the experiment was over, but never really turned out right. Only the ones who hadn't been separated from their mothers grew up to become normal, healthy monkeys.'

We were crossing the intersection at the Vrijheidslaan.

'Papa,' Bo said suddenly, 'Papa, there's a leprechaun in the bag.'

'Really?'

'Really.'

'How can you tell?'

'It's moving.'

'Really?'

'Really. The bag is moving.'

'Uh-oh.'

Beside Bo on the back seat was a plastic bag containing a chunk of wood that was growing little golden-yellow toadstools. 'Shall we take it home to show Mama?' I'd suggested. Bo had thought that was a good idea.

'Eeeeee!' Bo screamed suddenly. His shock shocked me, because Bo didn't shock easily. I turned around to see what was happening. I tried to grab the plastic bag.

'Aaaaieh!' Bo shrieked.

The very next moment we ploughed into the boot of a double-parked, shiny black BMW.

'A leprechaun?' said the stunned owner of the BMW, a half-eaten meatball sandwich still in his hand.

'A leprechaun?' puzzled the traffic cop.

'A leprechaun,' mumbled the driver of the tow-truck as he jacked the twisted front wheels of Monika's car off the ground.

I took the bag in one hand, Bo by the other. The Ceintuurbaan was within walking distance. At the house we took out the piece of wood. There was no leprechaun anywhere. But the toadstools were broken.

'There was a leprechaun, really,' Bo insisted stubbornly. 'I saw it.'

I was standing under the shower, rinsing the sweat

and the dirt and the fear off my body, when Bo poked his head around the shower door. 'Come here,' he whispered. He was holding a finger to his lips. 'The leprechaun's come back.'

I stepped out of the shower, dripping wet. The chunk of wood was lying on the coffee table. Beside the wood, a shrew was crawling around dazedly. Bo screamed with laughter. 'You see it? Look!' The terrified shrew crawled back into the dark hole where it had hidden while we were examining the toadstools in the woods.

'A leprechaun?' Monika said when she got home.

'Yeah, a leprechaun,' Bo said. 'Look.'

Monika groused at me for the next three days.

'We'll buy a bigger one,' I said.

'That's not the point.'

'A prettier one. Newer. One that's safer.'

'That's not the point.'

'Well, what is the point?'

'A car isn't a thing, a car is a place. Like a house. Its value is determined by the memories you have of that place.'

I said, 'To tell you the truth, it was all Bo's fault.'

No one could laugh as derisively as Monika.

13

Robbert Hubeek does not, as his address might lead one to believe, live in an upmarket area. He lives in the most run-down house in the most run-down section of a street that only half belongs to the most chic part of Amsterdam-South. He undoubtedly pays an exorbitant amount of rent (for the location), and undoubtedly awards the address a prominent place on his business cards (for the mistaken impression it creates).

'R. Hubeek & RPF Consultancy', the nameplate says. I ring the bell, which is mounted crookedly on the doorpost.

'Armin, my good man, is that really you?' Robbert had shouted into the phone when I called him. 'How nice to hear from you again.' I ignored his joviality.

'I need to talk to you,' I said. 'Lately I've been bothered a bit by memories of my time with Monika. There are a few things I can't remember very well any more, and I thought maybe you'd be able to throw a little light on them.'

'My heavens, poor boy!' he shouted. 'So she still won't leave you alone! But of course, you're always welcome. Talk about old times, with a drink and a cigar. Of course, of course, by all means, do drop in. What a surprise! To be honest, I haven't thought about the two of you for a

long time, about you and Monika I mean. And how is
that little one of yours – what's his name again?'

'Bo.'

'Oh, yes. Bo. Always did find that a peculiar name.'

'Fine,' I said. 'Bo is doing just fine.'

'Big by now, of course.'

'Yes, he's big.'

'Well, you'll have to tell me all about it. When would
you like to come round?'

His Filofax seemed to impose few limitations, because
actually, as he said himself, any time at all would be fine.
We agreed to meet late that afternoon. ('Then we can
have a little drink, although as far as I'm concerned we
can do that at eleven in the morning, too, ha ha ha!') It
also gave me a good excuse not to stay too long.

Robbert has to come down the stairs to open the door.
He stations himself pontifically in the doorway, arms
folded across his chest, a broad grin on his face.

'Well, well,' he says, eyeing me carefully. 'Age has not
passed you by entirely, I see. Even though one does one's
best to hide it.' He points a pale, fleshy finger at my
shoes. 'Red All-Stars. Haven't had those in my house
since Monika's day. Come in.'

He leads me up the stairs. Beige corduroy trousers,
leather slippers. His shirt-tails hang nonchalantly out of
his trousers, but fail to hide the fact that he still has no
arse at all. ('See what I mean?' Monika said when we ran
into him at a café one evening. 'I've made a great leap
forward in the arse department. If only for that reason,
I'd never go back to him.' But she'd had a good deal to

drink by then, and when she'd been drinking she wanted sex later on, and when she wanted sex she started paying me compliments.) There's no carpeting on the stairs, and the paint is peeling. There are deep gouges in the walls where oversized objects have been dragged up. Someone has drawn a star of David on the wall in black magic marker and written 'Fuck the Hicks, Ajax For Ever!' underneath.

'Please enter my humble abode,' Robbert says when we get to an open door off the first landing. The house smells of stale beer and cigar smoke, and is in other ways reminiscent of a student apartment. In the living room is a colossal couch, its brown corduroy upholstery covered in stains. Across from the couch, an equally colossal TV, and an oak club chair with ears. Empty beer bottles have been tossed everywhere. As have old newspapers, magazines, unopened mail, a TV guide from a young, swinging broadcasting company. In the bookcase are a few volumes commemorating a lapsed law study, a six-year-old Snoecks agenda, two shelves full of comic books, and a hardback edition of *The Discovery of Heaven* by Harry Mulisch. The only decoration on the wall is a framed cover from *Privé* magazine, with a blurred photo of Crown Prince Willem-Alexander and a flaxen-haired girl. 'REVEALING! The Prince's Secret Love. Will this blonde become our queen?'

I'm just about to say something about time standing still, but Robbert beats me to it. 'I know what you're thinking,' he says. 'The eternal student! Well, that's right. I'm studying the senselessness of life. And let me assure you, it's a damned fascinating subject. Between classes I amuse myself with a little consultancy, which occasionally generates a bit of hard cash – what more could a fellow want? Well, all right, some sweet nookie, but even in that my needs are met on occasion. And besides, you know better than anyone the problems that can bring with it. I mean the more intensive dealings with those of the feminine persuasion – how long ago did you two split up? Come on,' he says, before I have a chance to respond to his question. (Split up? Could it be that he really doesn't know . . . ?) He turns and walks back out onto the landing. There I see a second door which opens into a room that's been converted into a prim and proper office. Glass table, glass desktop, a computer, parquet floor, an abstract painting on the wall, black leather chairs with chrome legs.

'Who lets you consult on them, for God's sake?' I ask.

'Not so snippy, please,' he grins. 'Retailers. One-man operations. Foreign trading companies with names like Asia Trading International and Kabul Trans. A motley crew that I guide through the jungle of Dutch legislation and regulations. Just far enough to keep them happy, not far enough to let them get along without me.'

We return to the living room with the stained couch. 'What'll it be?' he asks. 'Whisky, vodka or beer?'

'Whisky.'

'A Glenfiddich for an old friend with a broken heart. In the afternoon I myself stick to the national addiction of our Russian friends. Cheers.'

We drink. I search for the right words to begin my interrogation, but once again he's too quick for me.

'So come on, out with it, what's bothering you? What are these memories that keep you from your well-deserved sleep?'

'Recently, I've been given reason,' I begin circuitously, 'to believe that I, during the years I was with Monika, after a manner of speaking, was not the only man in her life.'

'Ho, ha, as if I hadn't guessed!' Robbert crows. 'Did you find a letter she wrote but never, for reasons no longer to be uncovered, got around to posting? Are you being bothered by an anonymous caller who summons you from bed in the middle of the night and pants in your ear about what a sweet fuck Monika was, and how much he misses her? Ha ha ha!'

His pleasure at his own eloquence overwhelms him, and he pours himself another vodka as a reward. 'How about you? Drink up, by all means. No better remedy for a broken heart than deep alcohol narcosis.'

'What I want to know,' I say, 'is: did she ever speak to you about something like that? Did she ever mention anything along those lines?'

'Um, um . . .' He stares straight ahead, deep in thought. 'What did we talk about in those days? Most of the time we fought, I remember that. She was always spouting that left-wing, feminist crap. As far as that goes, I was pleased enough to lose her to you, I don't mind telling you that. My masculine pride was dealt something of a blow, but then you must understand that now better than you did then, ha ha ha.' He's looking straight at me, the grin on his face the same as the one he met me with at the door – a grin that awakens boundless aggression in me. It's the same grin, I realize now, he was wearing in that photo with Monika. What reason did he have then, at our party, in our house, to grin like that?

'Did you ever go to bed with her back then . . . ?'

'Back when she was fucking you? Of course, my good man. You were already fucking her when she was still with me, or at least when I thought she was still with me. How *could* you have forgotten?'

I should have counted on him bringing that up, but still . . . I suddenly feel very small, as if I've been caught red-handed.

'I regret that,' I say weakly. 'That it had to happen that way.' But I don't mean it, and he knows it, and he knows I know he knows. He tops up my glass again and lets a long silence settle in. On the floor above our heads, someone crosses the room with heavy tread.

'I'm going to tell you something,' he says then, 'that you won't like.' His voice sounds different. There's pent-up rage in it. But also a little quiet triumph. Vindictiveness. I can feel the Glenfiddich burning in my stomach.

'Do you remember that time I came to your party? How long was that after Monika and I split up? At least a year and a half, maybe two. She was a few months pregnant – I remember that, because she wasn't drinking any more. But still, strangely enough, that evening, there it was again, that animal attraction between male and female, one might say the oldest emotion on earth.'

Once again he looks straight at me. A terse, nasty little smile is playing around his lips. 'I can't even explain to you,' he goes on, 'how I noticed, but there it was.

Something in her look. Something in the way she touched me. It had been at least a year since she'd touched me of her own free will. As far as that goes, though, I can reassure you: once she'd worked up the courage to tell me she was fucking someone else, there was no more intimacy between us. No matter how I tried, no matter what sensible arguments I brought to bear – I reckoned I at least had the right to a decent farewell hump, but she wouldn't hear of it. I blamed you for that for ages.'

He empties his glass, fills it again. And then suddenly that grin is back on his face. 'That evening she walked me to where the night bus stopped. Did you know that?'

I didn't know that.

'We walked down the Ceintuurbaan. She let me put my arm around her. I was drunk, of course. And I was as horny as a . . . as a . . . That's what she said, too. "You're drunk," she said. "And you're horny." I swear, she started in about it herself. I said, "Yes, I want to fuck you. Really hard and real long." I hadn't had a fuck in months, I was in a bad way. She said, "That's impossible." I said, "That's possible." "That's impossible," she said. "But you know what might be possible . . ." And she pushed me into a doorway. It was next to a shoe shop, I remember that. A dark corner between the shop entrance and a door with bells for the flats up above. She jerked me off right there. I wanted her to blow me, but she wouldn't. Didn't matter. I don't think I've ever come as fast as I did in that doorway. A pity, actually. That it was over so soon. Does that answer your question?'

Again, that grin.

Later on, in the bar with Dees, I slam my fist down on the table in pure frustration. Causing a glass of beer to fall over. Causing the beer to run off the table. Causing a gigantic wet spot on my crotch. Causing me to become more furious than I already was.

'The son of a bitch! That arrogant arsehole! You should have seen him sitting there. When he's finally finished revealing nothing at all, he lights up a cigar. "How is that son of yours – God, what's his name again?" he asked me. The miserable bastard. He just abused the situation, that's all. Monika was completely unstable back then. Pregnant women are all like that. What a filthy pig!'

But Dees doesn't say a thing. Only when I've finished ranting, and when new beers are on the table, does he say, 'At least now you know he isn't Bo's father. Reason enough for a certain relief, I should say. And even if what he says is true, I reckon things like that do happen. Which of us has never done things we'd rather not know about ourselves? Would you like to confess your most venal sins before a jury of all the women you've ever been to bed with?'

'But I didn't ask to have Monika's most venal sins spouted all over me by some frustrated, cigar-smoking, vodka-guzzling fake consultant, did I?'

'Well, yes, you did.'

'I did?'

'Yeah.'

'Yeah, maybe I did.'

*   *   *

'So how do you two handle things with that child?'
Robbert had asked afterwards.

'What?' I asked.

'Well, if I understand you correctly, you two have
broken up. Do you raise the kid, or does Monika?'

So he really didn't know.

'I do,' I said.

'And what about Monika?' he asked.

I stood up, put on my coat and left.

'To tell you the truth,' Dees goes on, 'I believe fuck-all of
that story of his about being walked to the bus stop, or
that jerking off. Sounds too much to me like the ultimate
frustrated juvenile fantasy.'

I'm so glad Dees is my friend.

14

Death heralded its arrival the same way new life does: with nausea. On a chilly April morning (the magpies were working on their nest again) I was engrossed in the roles of alpha- and beta-adrenergic receptors in liver cells when Monika suddenly came into the room. She looked pale, and her lips felt cold when she kissed me.

'I don't feel well,' she said. 'Queasy. Headache. I'm going to bed right away.'

I made a pot of linden tea, but when I brought it in to her she was already fast asleep. I finished my correction work and Monika slept. I took Bo to the house of a friend he played with twice a week, and Monika slept. I picked him up again, and Monika slept. Early in the evening she finally woke up. She felt even worse than she had that morning. I made a fresh pot of tea and she drank two cups. Then she wobbled to the toilet, where she stayed for at least twenty minutes.

'I need to throw up, but I can't,' she said when she reappeared at last. Her face was ashen. She had dark rings under her eyes, and her usually buoyant hair hung in limp strands.

'You've got the 'flu,' I said.

'Yeah, and a whopper at that.'

'Mama has the 'flu,' Bo said.

'Fever?' I asked.

'I think so.'

I laid my hand on her neck, and felt her forehead, but she seemed cold rather than hot. A few minutes later the thermometer read 40.2. Monika shivered. I put another blanket over her.

'Mama has the 'flu,' Bo said. 'Mama needs to sleep.'

'That's right, Mama needs to sleep.'

I took him to the living room, tucked him up on the sofa with a pillow and the new Bert and Ernie duvet that Monika's parents had given him when he turned three.

'Read a book?'

'Yeah, let's read a book.'

'In a remote, narrow mountain valley,' I read aloud, 'somewhere far in the north of Scotland, sat Leta, a beautiful golden eagle, on her huge nest of branches and twigs. She was sitting on two big spotted eggs. They would be hatching soon, and she was pleased about that.' By the time the chicks had emerged from their eggs and father eagle had gone to nail a ptarmigan for his children, Bo was asleep. (That was back before his nightmares, back when he still slept with his eyes closed. His eyes slowly fell shut, popped open again in a last-ditch attempt to ward off sleep. But then sleep overpowered him at last, and he surrendered with a sigh – the loveliest moment of the day.) *Fulgor the Golden Eagle* and *Timur the Tiger* were Bo's favourite books, while the only thing he liked about *Kra the Baboon* was the cover, because it showed a wild leopard pouncing from a rock onto a baboon. Otherwise he thought it was a stupid book, although he couldn't explain why.

While Bo slept, I read on until I got to Fulgor's first
hunting lessons – Bo's favourite passage. 'Fulgor was
wild with happiness when he discovered his first mouse,'
I read. 'His legs held stiff in front of him, he dropped,
and suddenly he felt something soft and furry move in
a deathly struggle beneath his right talon. A second later
the little animal was dead, and for a few minutes the
young eagle toyed with it the way a cat does, rolling
it through the grass and seizing it again, then taking
it into the air for a moment and dropping it again,
until he finally decided to eat it, which he did at one
hungry gulp.'

Monika always said Bo was much too young for books
like that. But Bo didn't agree, and neither did I.

'Death is a part of life, Mo,' I told her. 'There's
nothing unusual or cruel about it. Before long Bo is
going to want a hamster, and animals like that die
much too fast, of course. So he might as well get used
to the fact that animals die. People, too.' (How was I to
know what was about to happen? Besides, I hadn't yet
read the verse from the Gospel of Philip that goes: 'In
this world there is good and evil. Its good is not good
and its evil not evil. But there is evil after this world
which is truly evil – what is called "The Middle". It is
death.' I never again read to Bo from *Fulgor the Golden
Eagle*.)

The next morning Monika still didn't feel better. The
fever had abated a little, but all the vitality seemed to
have been sucked out of her. She stared at me with
hollow eyes, and all she said was 'Jesus, I feel so rotten.'

She drank her tea, but only after a lot of coaxing. And she didn't want to eat.

'If you don't feel better by this afternoon, I'm going to call the doctor,' I said.

'Does Mama still have the 'flu?' Bo asked, a touch of disapproval in his voice.

'Yeah, Mama still has the 'flu.'

That afternoon the doctor came, but none too eagerly. ('Can't you wait a day and see how it goes?' 'No, I can't wait a day. I've never seen her like this.' 'What's her temperature?' 'I don't know, she's too sick to take it herself. But last night it was 40.2, and this morning it was 39.9.' 'What I would recommend is—' 'What I would recommend is that you come round this afternoon.' He came.)

I'd never met the man before, but I could tell he was shocked when he saw Monika. The testiness with which he'd shaken my hand disappeared immediately. He sat down on the edge of the bed and tried to talk to her. Her left arm lay white and fragile on the blankets. For the first time, I noticed there were little red spots on it.

'Monika?' the doctor said quietly. 'Monika?'

She didn't react right away. When it finally sank in that someone was calling her name, she opened her eyes just a crack. Her lips formed a word, but no sound came out.

'How are you feeling, Monika?'

'Bad,' we heard then, very softly.

'Do you have a headache?'

She nodded, almost imperceptibly.

'Nauseous?'

'Not any more.'

'Where does it hurt?' He laid his fingertips carefully on her right temple. 'Here?' She shook her head.

'Here? Or here?'

'Yeah.' A little to the left of centre.

'When did this start?' he asked me.

'Yesterday morning. She came home from work about ten thirty. She said she was nauseous. And she had a headache. She slept all afternoon. And almost the whole evening. And last night. And almost all day today. But it doesn't seem to make her feel any better.'

'I need to take her temperature,' the doctor said. 'We can do it orally.'

He took a thermometer out of his bag, tapped it against the palm of one hand and slid it into a plastic sleeve. 'Could I put this in your mouth, Monika?'

She opened her mouth. He inserted the thermometer. Simply closing her mouth again seemed to wear her out. The doctor remained seated, bending over her. He put his hand on her forehead again. Looked at her face.

'May I?' he said, and picked up her arm to study it carefully. As he waited for the mercury to rise, his eyes never left her for a moment. The way he gave her his undivided professional attention was reassuring and alarming, all at the same time. His 'tsk-tsk' when he read the thermometer was just plain alarming.

'It would be best, Monika,' he said, 'for you to go to hospital, just to be on the safe side. You might have a nasty infection. They can see that better in the hospital than we can here. And, more importantly, it will be easier for them to do something about it there. Do you have a car?' he asked me.

'Not any more.'

'Hmm. She's really too sick to take a taxi. Her temperature is almost up to 42. Could I use your phone?'

'Of course.'

I showed him the phone. He called the hospital, briefly explained the situation, and asked for an ambulance.

'No reason to be too concerned,' he said after he'd hung up. 'It was good that you had me come. But I need to rule out a few things. It seems to me that she's come down with an infection. That could be anything. The important thing is to find out where the infection's located. I need to be certain about that. If you like, you can go with her in the ambulance. I'll take the boy with me. I'll follow you there.'

He smiled, but without much conviction.

'Would you like that, Bo?' I asked.

Bo clutched my trouser leg and said nothing.

'We'll see,' the doctor said.

I went back into the bedroom and began putting some of Monika's things in a bag.

'Where's Mama going?' Bo asked.

'Mama's going to sleep over at the hospital.'

'Why?'

'Because she's sick. And because they can make her better faster there than they can here.'

'Oh,' Bo said. 'Are you going to the hospital, too?'

'Yes, but only to take Mama there. After that you and I are coming home.'

'Can I go with you?'

'Yes, but then you'll have to ride with the doctor. There isn't enough room in the ambulance for all of us.'

'I don't want to go with that man.'

'And what if I go with that man, too?'

Yes, then it was okay.

'Could we do that?' I asked the doctor.

'Sure.'

I told Monika what was going to happen. The trace of a smile appeared on her lips and she nodded, almost imperceptibly. When they lifted her into the ambulance, a choking fear seized me by the throat.

The doctor's car stank of cigarette smoke.

Last night I lay in bed thinking about that doctor – for hours. How well did he know Monika? I thought about how he'd put the thermometer in her mouth, how he'd laid his fingers on her forehead, how he'd spoken to her. Could it be? Is that why he came up with the suggestion that Bo ride with him, and I go in the ambulance? Had he wanted to be alone with his son, his illegitimate child, for a while? I waved those thoughts aside as ridiculous paranoia, dozens of times. There wasn't much chance that Bo's father (whoever that was) knew he was the father, though he may have suspected. But then again, how often did you read in the papers about doctors and their illicit relationships with patients?

By the time the first blackbird started singing, I was convinced I'd found the culprit, and that there was nothing for it but to locate him and confront him with my findings. For some reason I thought you could say things like that straight to a doctor's face, so there was no reason for the meeting to be as difficult and painful as the one with Robbert. (What's more, I didn't have to worry about being handed a pack of lies, invented for no reason other than revenge.) And, even if he turned out not to be the father, maybe he knew who was. Maybe Monika had confided in him; after all, his professional oath meant he had to keep it a secret. But that oath didn't apply any more, did it? I could always point out to him that the interests of a living boy took precedence over those of his dead mother, so Bo had a right to know who his father was – should he have any information along those lines.

This morning I leafed through the phone book. His office is still at the same address. I can see him Tuesday of next week. He sounded neither surprised nor suspicious. But I refuse to think about whether that means anything.

'Bacterial meningitis,' the doctor at the hospital had said.

'Is that serious?'

'It can be very serious. We'll just have to hope we're in time.'

'And if we're not?'

'If we're not, it can be fatal.'

They weren't in time. Monika lay in the hospital for three days. And every day she got worse. On the afternoon of the second day, she regained consciousness for a moment. I was beside her bed. She said, 'Armin, I'm going to die, aren't I?'

I said, 'No, Monika, you're not going to die. Of course you're not.'

'I'm going to die. I'm sorry.'

That was the last thing she said to me: 'I'm going to die. I'm sorry.'

Those three days were a nightmare. So was the week after that. The next two months I spent working like an idiot.

'Where's Mama?' Bo asked every now and again.

'Mama is dead,' I would tell him.

'Oh yeah. Mama's dead.'

Two years ago my mother died of intestinal cancer. She was seventy-two. My father phoned, at five thirty in the morning. 'Mama is dead,' he said. And I thought about Bo, and about Monika, and when the tears came I didn't know who I was crying for.

'She died peacefully,' my father said.

15

She's walking down the other side of the street. Her face and hands white as snow, her red hair like a warning.

'Look out!' she shouts.

I follow her gaze and see a little girl on my side of the street, standing at the kerb. She's trying to cross, but there's too much traffic. I walk over to her; she's about six, with short blonde hair and blue eyes that remind me of the first nice day in March.

'Come on,' I say, taking her hand. She doesn't seem afraid or surprised. She smiles at me. We cross the street together.

'Thank you,' she says when I take the child to her.

'My pleasure.'

On my way home, I can't stop thinking about her. Green eyes. Or were they grey? I've forgotten already. She had a nice voice. Self-assured, but friendly too. Soft, but not girlishly soft.

Two weeks go by, during which the memories fade. Then, suddenly, there she is again. The tram stops at the Leidseplein and she gets on. That white skin, that red hair. She moves up the aisle to a spot near me. Green eyes. Or more like greyish-green.

'How's the little blonde girl?' I ask. 'Is she more careful about crossing the street these days?'

She looks at me in surprise. Then bursts out laughing. 'My little neighbour girl, you mean? She's the kind of child who makes you want to ban all cars from the city, isn't she?'

She laughs and the tram shakes, but the one has nothing to do with the other, except in my mind.

'I'm surprised you recognized me.'

'Immediately.'

'My hair.'

'Your eyes.'

'Of course.' She laughs again. She has lovely, straight teeth.

'Where are you headed?'

'To the Bijenkorf, to do some shopping.'

'Can I go with you?' It's out before I know it, probably surprising me even more than it does her.

'You're a bit like my little neighbour girl,' she says.

The tram jerks and shakes heavily again. In the curve on the Spui she almost loses her footing. With one hand she grabs my coat and pulls herself back on balance.

'We could have a cup of coffee on the top floor. With apple pie,' I say.

'Oh, all right,' she sighs teasingly.

As we cross the Dam she walks close to me.

'I'm afraid of pigeons,' she says. I've never heard anything so preposterous. But I don't tell her that.

'What's your name, anyway?'

'Monika.'

'I'm Armin.'

'Ar-min,' she says, as if she's trying to taste the sylla-bles. 'Armin. That's different.'

In the restaurant at the Bijenkorf we drink coffee and eat apple pie with whipped cream. She tells me about her little neighbour girl. That they go out and do things together all the time; go to the park, to the museum when it's raining, to the zoo.

'What are her favourite animals?' I ask.

'The elephants.'

'Have you told her that elephants weep?'

'No. Do elephants weep?'

'They certainly do. Back in the Fifties there was a circus elephant called Sadie who didn't learn her tricks quickly enough. The elephant trainer punished her for her stupidity by beating her on the side of the head with a stick. To his amazement, she began crying, horribly, heartbreakingly. He never hit her again. And she was good and learned all her tricks.'

'And what if my little neighbour girl had a different favourite animal?' she asked. 'Would you have told me something about that one, too?'

'Sure. What's your favourite animal?'

She thinks about it. Then, with that mocking smile of hers that's already won my heart completely, she says, 'The goldfish.'

'The goldfish?'

'Yeah.'

I whistle through my teeth and laugh. 'In an alcohol solution of 3.1 per cent, a goldfish will lose its ability to swim upright within six to eight minutes.'

'That's a lie! You're making that up.'

'No, really. For years, goldfish were used to test the effects of alcohol on learning capacity. It seems that when you teach goldfish a trick in water laced with a little alcohol, they forget the trick when they're back in normal water, but they can repeat it once they're intoxicated again. Later on they tried the same experiment on people. And it worked exactly the same way.'

She looks at me, still dubious. 'And exactly what kinds of tricks did they teach those goldfish?'

'To swim simple mazes, for example. You don't believe me, but it's true.'

She says, 'You'd make a good father.' (I've never forgotten that. I'd just turned twenty and I'd never thought of myself as a potential father – being a father was something for my father, but certainly not for me. Her saying it just like that amazed me and excited me and moved me, all at the same time. And I thought, maybe my father's right: maybe it *is* time I started going after girls instead of watching birds.)

After we'd had our coffee, we went to the women's-wear department. She tried on two blouses, while I waited patiently at the entrance to the changing rooms, as though we'd known each other for years.

'How do you like this one?' she asked twice.

The first blouse didn't look good on her, and she saw that on my face before I could say anything.

'Oops,' she said. 'I get it.'

The second one looked lovely on her. 'You're absolutely gorgeous,' I said.

'Bullshitter.' Again, she laughed when she said it.

When I'd walked her to the tram stop, she asked, 'Don't you want my phone number?'

That's how it started. As unexpectedly as it ended.

16

During the eight weeks after Monika's death, I edited two hefty textbooks. One was about *Photosynthetic Mechanisms and the Environment*, the other was on *Pancreatic Islets*. When I take those books off the shelf now, it's as if I've never read them. Entire chapters deal with concepts I've never heard of. During those first eight weeks, the drunken filing clerk of my memory must have been lying in a coma.

When I go into the publishing house to deliver the final corrections on the book about the pancreas, Dees says, 'There's no more work for you for the next six months.'

'You're lying,' I say.

'You're right. But I want you to go home anyway. Call me if you need me, but I don't want to see your face around here for the next few months. There are all kinds of things you should be doing, but sitting around with your nose buried in manuscripts isn't one of them.'

I go home, make dinner, which we eat in front of the TV, put Bo to bed, read to him from Bert and Ernie (which he hates) and tell him to try to go to sleep, even if he isn't tired yet. Then I drink four glasses of whisky, lie down on the bed and stare at the ceiling until the pain in my eyes warns me that my corneas are drying out. I blink a few times, then start again.

At four in the morning I turn on the light in the living room. The park is still covered in nocturnal darkness, but on the eastern horizon a new day is dawning. The first blackbird sings the day. I walk over to the bookcase, close my eyes and run my finger across the spines. I take a book off the shelf without opening my eyes, sit down and open it.

I read, 'No one will hide a valuable object in something large, but many a time people have tossed countless thousands into a thing worth a penny. Compare the soul. It is a precious thing and it came to be in a contemptible body.'

I think about that until it's light outside. Then I put the book (which turns out to be an apocryphal gospel I didn't know Monika had) back on the shelf and get dressed. I wake Bo, slice bread and warm some chocolate milk, and put it all in a backpack. I dress him warmly and have him pull on his own gumboots. A little later we're walking hand in hand, into the still-silent city.

'Where are we going?' Bo asks.

'We're going to look for Mama.'

We walk down the Ceintuurbaan to the Amstel. On the bridge we stop to watch the birds. A grebe dives and comes back up with a fish in its beak. Bo claps his hands. The bird gulps down the fish and disappears under water again. Its body is so streamlined that it leaves barely a ripple. We don't see it surface again.

'Maybe it's got a nest down there,' Bo says, 'and now it's sitting on its eggs.'

Along the Weesperzijde, a frumpy blonde is letting out two Doberman Pinschers. Just to be safe, Bo moves around me and takes my other hand. At the Berlage Bridge we turn left. We wait under the trestle until a train comes over. Bo tilts his head all the way back and peers up.

'Maybe,' he says once the train has roared by, 'Mama is on the train.'

At Amstelstation I buy a day ticket, so we can travel as much as we want. While we're waiting on the platform for the first intercity train to Nijmegen, we drink some warm chocolate milk. A man in a suit and trenchcoat sits down beside us.

'Taste good?' he asks Bo.

Bo looks up at him, but says nothing. The man pulls a newspaper out of his briefcase. ('Moscow trembles,' the front page says. I'm glad Bo doesn't consort with people who read the *Algemeen Dagblad*.) When the train pulls in we wait until the man gets up and walks to the closest doors. Then we enter two doors further up.

'I saw Mama,' Bo says once we've torn past Holendrecht metro station, where the platform was filled with people on their way to work. He's sitting on my lap, peering intently out of the window.

'What did she look like?'

'She had on a green coat. And she had an umbrella.'

'Not like her to carry an umbrella when it's not raining,' I say.

'No,' Bo giggles, 'not like her, hee hee.'

At the station in Utrecht we see Monika again. She's stepped down off the train opposite and is walking towards us across the platform. This time she's wearing a denim jacket, and instead of an umbrella she's carrying a duffel bag made of Indian fabric from Guatemala or Mexico. Pinned to her jacket is a badge with a picture of Che Guevara. Her red hair stands up straight and short. She's just come from the hair salon. When she walks past our window I squint and watch her through my lashes – that way the illusion won't be destroyed.

'Her hair's awfully short,' Bo says.

I want to ask him if he thinks she's pretty, but no sound comes out.

'What happened to that pigeon?' Bo asks.

In the sand at the foot of a broad, low pine lie the remains of a wood pigeon. That is to say, its feathers.

'It was eaten by a hawk,' I tell him.

'What's a hawk?'

'It's a bird of prey. Sort of like Fulgor the Golden Eagle, but smaller.'

'Why don't you ever read to me from *Fulgor the Golden Eagle*?' Bo asks. Then he answers the question himself: 'Because Mama thinks I'm too little.'

'That's right,' I say. 'Because Monika thinks you're too little for that.'

We're on the heath at Planken Wambuis, but there's no sign of Monika here. We've had our sandwiches and finished the last of the chocolate milk, and now Bo is starting to get tired. He says, 'I want Mama to come back.'

'Mama isn't coming back. But she's not really gone, either.'

'Mama is dead!' he says angrily and kicks at the pigeon feathers with his little boot.

'That's right,' I say. 'Monika is dead. But we'll still see her a lot.'

'I don't want to see her any more.'

I don't know what to say to that. I pick him up and give him a piggyback. From the way his little body is shaking, I can tell he's crying. By the time we've crossed the heath and reached the edge of the woods, he's fallen asleep. I gently lower him to the ground, with his back against the trunk of a birch. I spread my coat out on the moss. Bo is awake.

'Come and lie down next to me,' I say.

We fall asleep beside each other, in the sun. The last thing I hear is the plaintive mewing of a buzzard.

In my dream I'm walking down a silent street that seems to have no end. I look into the windows, and in every house I see people sitting at tables. Men, women and children. Each house is furnished differently, but still all the houses look alike. Everywhere the table is in exactly the same place. Everywhere a man is sitting at the head of the table; the woman and three children are seated differently – but it's always two boys and a girl. The people are as different as people are, but in some strange way they all look alike, too: the parents are all the same age, so are the children. When I walk by they look up from their plates and stare at me as I pass. I'm walking down the even-numbered side of the street. When I first notice the numbers on the houses, I'm at number 26. By the time I get to number 244, the end of the street is still nowhere in sight. I walk faster all the time. I hardly dare look inside any more, but at the same time I can't stop. Always those five faces looking up from their plates: a man, a woman, two sons and a daughter. A man, a daughter, a woman and two sons. Suddenly I hear someone weeping. I look around, but there's no one else on the street. I peer into the house where I just stopped. Again, the five faces. But no one's crying. The weeping grows louder. Then I wake up with a start. The weeping is coming from Bo.

'Bo! What's wrong?'

He's lying on his stomach, his fists clenched under his face.

'I . . . I . . . I had such a scary dream.'

'What did you dream?'

'That I fell off the world.'

'You fell off the world?'

'Yeah. The world was square. And really far away. And I fell. I kept falling further away from the world.'

I help him sit up and hold him close. He's still sobbing a bit, and he sniffs hard a few times. I give him my handkerchief.

We sit there like that for a while without saying anything. I look at the buzzard still hanging high in the air above the heath. It circles on motionless wings. Whenever I see a buzzard I wish that I could glide that quietly, looking down on the world.

What a strange dream, I think. That he fell off the

world. The oppressive weight of my own dream has vanished.

'Shall we get going?' I ask. Bo is sitting on the edge of my coat, bent over something. A tiny little clump of person beneath a high Ruysdael sky.

'What are you doing?'

'Nothing.'

I sit up and look at what he's doing. He's pulling apart an owl pellet with his little fingers.

'Look,' he says. He holds up a minuscule piece of bone, with two sharp little teeth attached to it.

'The upper jaw of a mouse,' I say.

'Is this poop?'

'No. It's a pellet.'

'What's that?'

I explain it to him.

'Was it fun in the owl's stomach?' Bo asks the mouse's jaw. 'No, it wasn't, was it? You should have kept your eyes open.'

We pull the rest of the pellet apart and find another fragment of a mouse's skull, the remains of feathers and tiny bones that could belong to mice or birds.

'What's this?' Bo asks.

He's holding a black oval object between his fingers. 'That's a beetle shell,' I say. There are more casts lying around the tree where Bo found this one.

'From the looks of it, I'd say it was a wood owl,' I say. The pellets are elongated and irregular, with a point at one end, like most owl casts. They seem too big for a long-eared owl, and there aren't any short-eared owls around here. 'Maybe he's up in this tree.'

We look up. Bo is the first to spot the bird. It's sitting pressed up against the trunk, its plumage blending in almost completely with the bark. One of its round eyes is open and staring down at us insistently.

'He's awake!' Bo whispers.

We stand there and watch for a while. The owl closes its eye again.

'Hee hee,' Bo giggles. 'Sleep tight.'

It's twelve o'clock and I'm hungry. Monika would have known a good place around here to have lunch. She knew the best addresses all over the country – and she always refused to tell me how she'd acquired that knowledge. But we don't come across Monika in the woods. We follow a muddy path until we get to a paved road. A white marker says it's 2.1 kilometres to Ede.

We have Dutch pancakes with apple and treacle. Bo has ice cream for dessert, I order coffee and cognac. Bo's ice cream has a little paper umbrella sticking out of it.

'Hey, that's Mama's umbrella,' he says.

Outside the sun has gone back behind the clouds. The waitress, a girl with a fringe and pigtails and pimples on the back of her neck, comes to light the little candle in the middle of the table.

'How do you like that ice cream?' she asks Bo in a childish voice.

'That's my mother's umbrella,' he replies.

'I don't think your mother would fit under that umbrella.'

'Oh yeah, easily. 'Cos my mother's dead.'

The girl hurries away.

While Bo eats his ice cream, I silently stare at the yellow flame. When he's finished, I wipe his face.

'Where are we going now?' His fatigue has disappeared completely.

'Wherever you want.'

He frowns, a wrinkle of deep thought across his forehead. 'I want to go to Roermond.' Monika's parents live in Roermond. 'Then Grandma Paradies can cook for us tonight.'

'That's a good idea.'

In the vestibule I drop two coins into the phone and call Monika's parents.

'Hello, Paradies speaking,' her father says.

'Hello, this is Armin. How are you?'

'Armin' is all he says.

'Bo would really like to come over for supper tonight.'

'Bo wants to come to supper,' he repeats, apparently speaking to his wife. I hear her say that it's okay.

'Okay.'

'See you this evening, then.'

'Yeah.' He hangs up.

I haven't spoken to them since the funeral, and I realize that I have no idea what to say to them.

'You do the talking later on,' I say to Bo.

'What?'

'Tonight, at Grandpa and Grandma Paradies's house, you do the talking.'

17

On my desk is a piece of paper with a list of questions.

Why?

Was it passion?

Was it love?

Was it revenge?

Was it lust?

Was it boredom?

Was she drunk?

Was she angry?

Where was she?

Was she outside?

Was she inside?

What did she have on?

What did she take off?

Was the light on?

Was it dark?

Was there foreplay?

Was there afterplay?

Did she come?

Sometimes I find that I get excited when I think about those questions. Then I hate myself.

18

'**M**r Minderhout?'

The doctor sticks his head through the waiting-room door. I put down the copy of *Privé* in which I've been reading about Mel B's lovechild. Lovechild, I think. Was Bo a lovechild?

When I step into his office he's standing beside the desk, his hand held out in greeting.

'Mr Minderhout, it's been a long time.'

He's wearing tortoiseshell spectacles and his hair has turned grey. He must be well into his fifties by now. When he sits down in his chair I hear something in his knees go crack.

'Ten years,' I say.

'Take a seat, what can I do for you? Or rather, first let me ask, how is the little boy? Bo, wasn't it?'

'That's right, Bo. He's not so little any more.'

'How old is he?'

'Thirteen.'

'Thirteen. A difficult age. But he's doing well?'

'Yes, he's doing well.'

'And you?'

'Are you Bo's father?'

'Excuse me?'

'I asked whether you're Bo's father.'

He looks at me perplexedly. Then, not taking his eyes off me for a moment, he says very slowly: 'You're asking me . . . whether I'm . . . Bo's father?'

'Yes, that's what I'm asking.' Is he shocked? No, I don't think so – or else he's a master at hiding his emotions. Doctors are probably well versed in that. But, on the other hand, amazement *is* written all over his face.

'The answer to that,' he says, 'is no. But perhaps you could tell me why you think, or suspect, that I'm your son's father?'

'Because *I'm* not. So someone else must be.'

'You're not Bo's father?'

'No. I have Klinefelter's Syndrome. I'm sterile. Always have been.'

He purses his lips, ejects air from his lungs. 'Phhhewww.'

'For the last few years I've had a girlfriend. We wanted quite badly to have children. It turned out we can't.'

'My God,' the doctor says. 'And now you're looking for the father. For the man who . . .'

'That's right.'

'And you thought . . .'

'Yes. Why not?'

'Yes, indeed, why not? It *does* happen. The doctor–patient relationship can be very close, and we read in the papers all the time about how that that can get out of hand.' He picks up a glass paperweight and rolls it between his fingertips.

'Mr Minderhout,' he says then, 'I give you my word of honour that there was never anything untoward between your late girlfriend and myself. She was also decidedly not a person who tried to steer things in that direction.'

'Did she ever say anything to you, back then, when she came for her pregnancy check-ups? Confess anything?'

'No, never. My God. It's only now dawning on me what this must mean to you. I'm very sorry. I didn't see all the consequences right away.'

'Are you sure she never said anything?'

'Yes, absolutely. I would definitely remember something like that. I have a good memory, insofar as a person's memory can be good. But you probably know all about that by now.'

He opens a folder that's been lying on the table all this time. He looks at the index card with Monika's medical history, flips through the papers. I see the letterhead of the hospital where Monika died. He sighs.

'This must reopen a lot of old wounds for you.'

But I don't want to talk about that. I'm not looking for pity. 'If you can't help me any further,' I say, 'then I'm sorry to have bothered you. So I can take you at your word when you tell me you're not Bo's father?'

'You'll have to. I could tell you – but, no, I won't burden you with that . . . what's happened in my practice through the years. No one's hands are entirely clean, Mr Minderhout. Mine aren't, either, although fortunately it's never got to the point where . . . But, as far as Monika is concerned, I can look you straight in the eye: never, ever, did anything along those lines transpire between her and myself. And I am also not your son's father.'

I get up. 'Thank you. And should you reconsider . . .'

'I can't reconsider. There's nothing *to* reconsider. But do you mind if I ask you something?'

I already have my hand on the doorknob. He's standing up now, beside his desk again, holding his hand out to me as if I'd just come in the door.

'Have you told your son about this?'

'No. Is that all?'

'Yes. Yes, please excuse me. Of course, it's none of my business.'

I leave him standing beside his desk with his hand held out, and close the door behind me.

19

Monika's parents have always blamed me for her death, although I don't know why. Maybe they couldn't accept the idea that no one was to blame for their only child living only to the age of twenty-five. They aren't the kind of people to blame the doctors. There was no questioning authority, especially not the kind that wore white coats. (They had wanted Monika to go to medical school, but instead she chose cultural anthropology, and quit that after the first year. Her parents blamed me for that, too.)

In their eyes, the only good thing that I'd ever done, or at least that they thought and I thought and everyone thought I'd done, was to beget Bo. When Bo was born they were both still in their late forties, but their fondest wish was to be grandparents.

'They're pleased that they finally have a boy to ruin,' Monika said. 'It's what they always wanted. A daughter was only second best.'

For Monika's parents, having only one child wasn't a matter of free choice, the way it had been with mine. (My mother thought thirty-nine was too old for a second child, and my father never seemed to want a second one very badly. He'd proved what he was capable of. That was enough for him.)

'My parents went to every doctor in the country,' Monika said. 'But they never found a cause. Back then, of course, doctors couldn't do what they can today.'

One afternoon, when her parents were visiting us and had finished criticizing our small flat, and the way we took Bo everywhere we went, and our rather piddling employment, and our lack of material possessions, and our political opinions, and our views on marriage – when at last there was nothing left to criticize and they were just about to leave, her mother suddenly said, 'If I was still young, I'd have IVF. Then I could have a little boy, too.'

That night Monika lay in my arms and wept. And I said to Bo, 'Make sure you stay away from those creepy people.' But of course he didn't listen to me. Grandpa and Grandma Paradies became his favourite grandparents.

'So, little fellow,' Monika's mother says to Bo, 'Did your father finally work up enough courage to face us again?'

But Bo doesn't hear her. He's already on his way to the little room off the kitchen, where Grandpa Paradies is working on a model of a Dutch East India Company ship. He leaves a trail of sand on the newly polished floor. In a minute he's bound to knock over the model ship or create even greater havoc, but they won't be angry with him, not his favourite grandma and grandpa. They're only angry with me. As a matter of principle. Or out of cowardice. But that's usually the same thing.

'Hello,' I say to the woman at the door, and she kisses me stiffly and with palpable reluctance.

'Hello,' I say to the back of the man seated at the table, but he doesn't hear me, he listens only to his grandson telling him something about a gold coin and pirate treasure and about the taste of sand. (The street close to the railway station had been dug up. Bo had seen something glittering in the yellow sand. It turned out to be a chocolate coin, and he insisted that he be allowed to eat it. The sand had crackled between his teeth.)

The visit lasts four hours and thirty-five minutes. We talk a little. We eat a little. We laugh a little. When I ask how they've been getting on since the funeral, they don't answer me. About me and how I'm getting on they ask nothing at all. Only about Bo do they want to know everything there is to know, and the less I say the more questions they ask, and the more questions they ask the more I want to go away, away from this horrible house with its walls of brick siding and its false beams on the ceiling and its fake Dutch masters and its framed diplomas from the retail-trade school and the butchers' school and the yellowed awards from the trade federation for the meat and poultry branch, and that one photograph, that one photograph I can't look at but have to keep looking at – that photo showing Monika as a angelic girl, her red hair neatly combed, the edges of the picture blurred in a romantic soft focus. ('I was thirteen and had just lost my virginity. I hate that picture,' Monika said. But of course not when her parents were around.)

*   *   *

After that last visit they came to Amsterdam a few times. But when I kept refusing to honour those visits with a return one, they finally sent me an outraged letter.

'We want nothing more to do with you. You've taken from us the dearest thing we've ever had: our little Bo. We hope that when he's old enough he will defy his father and renew contact with us. He will always be welcome, but we'll never let you darken our door again.'

Only then, only after I had read that letter and reread it, after I had torn it into little pieces and burned it in the sink – only then did the tears come. That they hadn't said a word about Monika, that they'd called Bo the dearest thing they'd ever had, that's what finally broke the shell I'd built around myself.

I cried until there were no more tears. And then I cried a lot more.

20

Niko Neerinckx lives in Haarlem, with a wife and three young children, two boys and a girl. He's still off on trips all the time, but not for a travel agency; these days he works for idealistic organizations who do good things for humanity in faraway countries, and who want to publicize that fact by means of the most modern media. Niko Neerinckx has his own video-production firm, called Wandering Eyes. (Detective work is a grind, but also surprisingly easy. I wouldn't mind making a living at it.)

This morning I decided to meet his wife, before I confront him. It was a decision born more or less of necessity, because Niko's in Borneo for three weeks – as one of his helpful co-workers at Wandering Eyes told me. But the decision also makes my heart beat faster and my hands go clammy. Since the fruitless visit to Monika's old doctor, I've become increasingly convinced that Nico Neerinckx is the man I'm looking for. I have three reasons to believe that, which I duly noted in my pocket diary the day I located him. They read as follows:

N. N. was exciting.
N. N. was safe (regularly out of the country).

N. N. had a predilection for engaged or married women.

Now that I know he's not at home, and that I can get to know his wife before meeting him again, all kinds of wild scenarios race through my mind. The visit to Robbert Hubeek showed me the importance of working out whether you're being lied to. For starters, I must now make sure that Mrs Neerinckx (whose first name is Anke) doesn't know my true identity, so that Mr Neerinckx (Niko) won't know I've spoken to her. That way I can lay their stories side by side, and easily pick out any lies on his part. And if he *is* lying . . . The mere thought immediately summons up the most horrendous fantasies of revenge. But things haven't reached that point yet. I must remain calm. Think clearly. Stay keen. I must devise a strategy to get her talking. To that end, I lock myself up in my study for a few hours with a thermos of strong coffee. By the time the coffee's finished, I know exactly what I have to do.

I tell Ellen I'm going out that evening for a drink, with Dees. I know she worries about my renewed taste for alcohol, that she's afraid it will become as bad as it was the year after Monika died – the year she saved me from. But I need the periodic narcosis of alcohol to keep me on my feet, and to provide me with the excuse of popping off to a bar. It's as if I'm pushing Ellen and Bo away, to make room for what's coming, for what *has* to come if I'm not to go mad from despair and bewilderment.

The weather, to my delight, turns horrible in the course of the afternoon. Lead-grey clouds chase low across the city and the wind whips hail and rain against the windows, flogging cyclists and pedestrians. This considerably improves my chances of being let in, at least for a moment, by Mrs Anke Neerinckx. (I was surprised by that, to find she went by the name of Neerinckx – it always surprises me when women my age give up their own names for those of their husbands. I've made Ellen solemnly swear not to do that, otherwise I'll never marry her. But perhaps Anke Neerinckx's maiden name was something burdensome, like Fokking. One must never be too quick to judge. In any event, her voice on the phone sounded clear and self-assured. 'Excuse me, I'm trying to reach the Demircioglu family,' I said. 'There's no one here by that name,' she said. 'I'm very sorry, I must have dialled the wrong number. Is this . . .' And I read her number aloud, changing only the final digit. 'No,' she said. 'This number ends in a five, not a four.' 'Oh, I'm very sorry.')

When I'm finally on the train to Haarlem, after forcing down my dinner, a benevolent calm settles over me. Tonight I will do only what I *must* do, without hesitation, and with a boldness that was last mine that first time I met Monika on the tram, and asked to go with her to the Bijenkorf. Tonight I will take my life back into my own hands. Perhaps, I muse, that will be the end purpose of this nightmare: to shake me out of the half-slumber I've been in so long, in fact, ever since Monika died.

I watch the new office buildings and factories in the western harbour area as they're slowly swallowed up by the fall of darkness, and I say (so loudly that the woman across the aisle glances over at me), 'This is your wake-up call from the far shore of the River Styx.'

Standing in a doorway across the street, I can see the lighted windows of the Neerinckx house. Mother is putting the children to bed. At least, that's what I assume I'm seeing. A floor lamp is on in the living room, but the room is empty. Three windows on the top floor were lit just a moment ago, but now there are only two: one little window belonging to what is probably a toilet or a shower, the other to a bedroom. The curtains are closed, but a band of light is shining through a crack and the fabric gives off a faint glow. Every once in a while I see a shadow move across the yellowish-green field. Then the bathroom window suddenly becomes a black hole. A moment later a woman appears in the living room. She walks to the back of the room and disappears from sight. Less than a minute later, she reappears, a mug in her hand. Her dark hair is pinned up. She's wearing a green sweater and black trousers or a skirt, I can't quite see which. She sits down on a couch against a long wall straight across from the window. Carefully, she takes a sip. Then another. She gets up and closes the curtains (they're trousers, not a skirt). The curtains are off-white. For a moment I see her shadow, then nothing.

The wind is still blowing hard, but it's stopped raining. I decide to walk around the neighbourhood for fifteen minutes. It's a few minutes past eight, so she's probably watching the news. During the weather report seems a more propitious moment to ring the bell. Besides, that will give me time to run through my story one last time.

Circumstances have dropped a unique opportunity right in my lap, and I mustn't blow it.

'Good evening, my name is Aldenbos, Erik Aldenbos.' 'Good evening, sorry to disturb you.' No, not disturb. 'Sorry to bother you like this.' No, better introduce myself first, that forges a bond of trust. 'Good evening. Aldenbos is the name, Erik Aldenbos.'

'Good evening, I'm Erik Aldenbos. Sorry to just show up at the door like this, but I couldn't find your name anywhere, so I couldn't phone first.'

I hadn't been planning to say that, but when I eventually got to the portico I looked around and didn't see a nameplate anywhere, so when Anke Neerinckx opened the door that line just rolled off my lips.

She looks at me questioningly, the door open only far enough to get a good look. She's switched on the light in the portico, and I blink my eyes in the glare. Suddenly I'm afraid that will make me look untrustworthy.

'I used to live here,' I say quickly. 'As a child. Years ago. Something happened then. Well, it's a long story. What it all boils down to is that I hid a letter in the attic. And that letter, well, as I said, it's a long story, but my mother died recently and I suddenly remembered that letter, and I thought, wouldn't it be great if I found it? And then I thought, why not just try? So here I am.'

I spread my arms helplessly and smile at her.

'Here, in our attic?' she says.

'That's right. Between two rafters. It was hidden pretty well. We moved rather unexpectedly back then, and I forgot to take it. By the time I remembered it, I didn't have the courage to bother the new owners. There are a lot of things you dare to do when you're a kid, but not when you're an adult. But then there are also a lot of things you don't dare to do when you're young, and later you think, what do I have to lose?'

She smiles, but I still don't have her quite where I want her. She says, 'It would have been better if you'd come during the day.'

'Of course, you're right,' I say. 'I wasn't really planning to ring the bell. I was looking for a nameplate, as I said, so I could phone first.'

'Our name is on the mailbox, on the garden fence. Neerinckx. With ckx.'

'Oh, excuse me!' I glance at the green mailbox on the garden fence. If I'd only been looking for their name, I would never have missed it. I should have stuck to the lines I'd learned and not started prattling about some nameplate. I feel my resolve crumbling.

'Could I,' I ask, 'ring you tomorrow, perhaps?' I feel ridiculous. A liar. Tomorrow I won't even have the nerve to ring. I'm convinced of that.

'That would be better, yes. I'll write down the number for you.'

She's about to walk back down the hall, but the wind blows the door open behind her and she turns around to catch it. I see her hesitate; she's too well brought up, too kind, to close the door in someone's face.

'Please, come inside,' she says. 'The weather's so horrible.' And she smiles and holds the door open for me. I walk past her into the hall. As soon as I'm over the threshold, I feel my confidence returning.

'I was just watching the news, the beginning of the weather report. I don't think they're expecting it to get any better for a few days.'

I can't see the television from where I'm standing, but I can hear the weatherman's familiar voice. Anke Neerinckx goes to the kitchen from where she'd fetched the cup of coffee or tea I'd seen earlier, and comes back with a notepad and a pen.

'These blue areas on the radar,' the weatherman says, 'show that we're experiencing some heavy squalls here and there, with rain and even some occasional hail. Those squalls are going to increase in intensity during the night, and the wind will pick up as well.'

At that very moment a gust hits the living-room window like a big, flat hand. There's a roaring that slowly swells to a loud clatter, then blends into a sharp, ticking sound. It's hailing again. Anke Neerinckx walks over to the window, pushes aside the curtain and sighs.

'Miserable weather,' she says. 'Here's our number.'

I'm still standing in the doorway between the hall and the living room. She hands me a scrap of paper with the phone number I already have. 'Thank you, Mrs Neerinckx,' I say.

'Call me Anke. It makes me feel so old when people say Mrs Neerinckx.'

'I know how that is. Sir, that's the worst. When people start calling you sir.'

Outside the hail pounds against the window again.

'If you ring me late tomorrow morning, I'll definitely be at home.'

'You've done a fine job renovating the old place. Or was it like this when you moved in?'

She looks around the room. 'No. Oh, no, we did this. There was a wall here. It was two rooms, one in front, one at the back, and the hall ran all the way back to the kitchen. But of course I don't have to tell you that.'

'It must have been a very small living room. But I never saw it that way as a child.'

'Children take the world as it comes.'

'When you're a child, the grown-up world is a huge place.'

I make a move to leave.

'Anyway, sorry to have disturbed you.'

'How far do you have to go? Do you live here in Haarlem?'

'No, in Amsterdam. I had dinner with an old friend of mine here in town. Another connection with that letter business. But I'd better get down to the station.'

'Yes. I don't mean to be stuffy, it's not that I don't trust you or anything,' she says, 'but I have three little children sleeping upstairs. If they suddenly heard footsteps in the attic, they'd be terrified. It would take me hours to get them back to sleep.'

'Three,' I say. 'That's nice. How old are they?' She tells me their ages (one and a half, three and five) and their names (Pim, Sam and Bo).

'Bo!'

'Yes.'

'Well . . . well, that's quite a coincidence.' I'm about to say: that's my son's name too, and a lot more, but I don't. Bo! Christ! They named their oldest son Bo!

'A friend's son,' I say, in order to say anything at all. 'In fact, the friend I went out to dinner with tonight. His son's name is Bo, too. I was just telling him that I didn't realize it was a boy's name. I only knew of Bo Derek.' I'm amazed at how quickly the lies roll off my tongue tonight. But the end justifies the means. I'd already decided about that.

'I had the same thing, you know,' she says apologetically. 'And I despise Bo Derek. It was my husband's idea. And he swore to me that it had nothing to do with Bo Derek. He said it was a boy's name, actually. And the agreement was that, if it was a boy, he'd choose the name. If it was a girl, I'd choose. That's how it happened. Sam was my idea. *He* claimed that was a boy's name. So we divvied it up pretty evenly.'

She must have noticed how uncomfortable I am, but she probably thinks it's because I'm still standing in her doorway with my coat on. For the first time in my life, though, I'm experiencing what it's like to be nailed to the spot.

Bo. It was my husband's idea.

She says, 'If you'd like to wait until the rain lets up a little, feel free to sit down. Shall I take your coat? Would you like a cup of coffee?'

'Yes, yes please, yes.'

I'm glad to be able to get off my feet, pleased that she's left the room for a moment.

'What do you take in it?' she calls from the kitchen.

'Nothing. Black, thanks.'

On TV a little boy in a football strip is doing a dance of joy on the field. He's paid careful attention to how his professional heroes act when they score a goal. The commercial (for a brand of peanut butter) is endearing, even if you don't have children of your own, even if your son isn't your son, but the son of the man whose wife just handed you a cup of coffee.

Christ!

I'll have to leave my coffee until my hands stop shaking a bit. I want to get out of here. I want to search the whole house, from top to bottom. I want to run down the street, into the rain, into the night, jump into the dark water of the River Spaarne. I want to wake her children to see how much they look like Bo. I want to tell Anke Neerinckx that her husband is a liar, an adulterer, the father of a bastard, a pervert who names his oldest son after the child he sired by another man's wife. I want to lay my head on her breast and beg her to hug me, to stroke me, to take me to bed and sleep with me. I want to smack her up against the counter where she's making coffee for me, yank down her black sweatpants and rape her till she bleeds.

'Aren't you feeling well?' she asks, sounding startled.

'Excuse me?'

'You look so pale.'

'I think,' I say dully, 'it's the sudden change, from cold to warm. I have low blood sugar.' As good an excuse as any.

'Shall I put some sugar in your coffee?'

'No, no, thank you.'

'A piece of chocolate? Does wonders. After three pregnancies, I should know.'

She smiles at me. She has a lovely smile. Niko Neerinckx married a lovely woman. But I'd have expected nothing less. Anke is the kind of woman I would once have filed away as unattainable. Too beautiful. The kind of beauty a lot of men go for, but the kind most of them also find intimidating. For Niko, she must have been the ultimate challenge. I bet she was involved with someone else when he met her.

I take a piece of chocolate. She turns off the TV and settles down on the other half of the corner couch, in the spot where I saw her drinking coffee earlier. That it could be so easy! That I would find out what I needed to know so quickly! My head is still spinning, but fortunately she doesn't notice. She nestles down cosily amid the soft cushions of the couch, like a cat, her legs pulled up under her.

'So tell me, what was the story about that letter?'

21

For Rotterdam we make an exception, otherwise the city would cease to exist. But for the rest of the country we show no mercy: everything from after 1945 has to go.

'See that petrol station? Kiss it goodbye! That office block? Blow it up!'

Quonset huts, viaducts, electricity sub-stations, housing estates, warehouses, on-ramps, off-ramps, phone booths, hardware stores, apartment buildings, bus stops, traffic lights, golf courses, control towers, ski slopes, billboards, ranch-style housing, middle schools, go-kart tracks, holiday villages, pig farms, ministries – raze, tear down, destroy!

We're sitting in the train and we're cleaning up the Netherlands.

'What shall we put there instead?' Bo asks.

'For that road there, grassland. For that office building, a farm. For that housing estate, market gardens.'

We dig old ditches anew. Give rivers room to run. We tear neon signs and decorative awnings off old buildings. We renovate classic shopfronts, putting leaded glass back in the windows and adding hardwood sills. We plough kilometres of asphalt under the Dutch clay.

Research for policy. Forget it. *Nokia copiers.* Away with it.

'Where are we going?' Bo had asked.

'Back in time. To the Holland Grandpa grew up in.' In 1940 my father had just turned thirteen, twice as old as Bo is on this glorious spring day.

'We'll repopulate the ditches,' I tell Bo halfway between Leiden and The Hague. 'Now that the ground is no longer over-fertilized, the water is clear and whole-some.'

'There should be big fat pike in it,' Bo says.

'And rock bass,' I say.

'Water-stick bugs.'

'Sticklebacks.'

'Diving beetles.'

Bo has a predilection for robbers and bandits. The water-stick bug, which lies motionless just beneath the water's surface, breathing through its snorkel, on the lookout for other water bugs which it kills with one snap of its powerful jaws. The diving beetle, bold enough to take on fish three times its size. And its equally voracious larvae, not averse to devouring the occasional salaman-der. (They use their hollow jaws to inject intestinal juices into their prey, then suck them dry.)

'Minnows,' I say.

'Water spiders,' Bo says.

'Pond skaters.'

'Whirligig beetles.' (The whirligig uses the top half of its eyes to watch the sky, ready to dive when danger approaches; with the other half it peers down into the water, searching for edible passers-by. When it dives, it takes a bubble of air with it to keep from drowning. Impeccable design, on the head of a pin.)

'Black terns can nest here again.'
'And storks can walk around.'
'There won't be as many blue herons, though.'
'Doesn't matter.'
'No, that doesn't matter.'

In The Hague we pull ten thousand cars off the road.

'What kind of cars were there in the 1930s?'

The Peerless V16, with its 7.6-litre engine and that long, gleaming bonnet. On Matheneserplein in Rotterdam you could see them through the window of the show-room of Peerless Motor Imports, which shipped them in from Cleveland, Ohio. The Peerless was so expensive and so exclusive that in the late 1930s there were only thirty-eight of them on the road in Holland. When President Roosevelt put an end to Prohibition and alcoholic drinks could once again be sold legally all over the United States, the manufacturer of the Peerless switched to brewing – there was more money in that.

'What else?'

Rapides from Belgium. Built in Antwerp, designed by Amsterdam engineer Silvain de Jong. The cheapest model was the 12hp, which sold for 5,400 guilders. In 1936 the Rapide factory went bust owing to the brutal competition from American motor companies, Ford in particular.

'How much did a Ford cost'

You could buy a Ford V-8 for as little as 1,025 guilders. The convertibles were a little more expensive: 1,190 guilders and up. For 135 guilders extra you got a built-in car radio. When the war broke out, there were

937 Fords on the road here. Other carmakers could only dream of sales like that.

'It must have been really quiet on the streets,' Bo says.

'In a lot of villages,' I say, 'you could drive through only if the local constable walked along in front of you, to warn pedestrians.'

'Did Grandpa's family have a car?'

'Grandpa Minderhout's didn't. But the Paradies family's did. And Grandpa Paradies's mother owned a motorbike. She was the first woman in Holland with a motorbike.'

'Too bad we never see them any more, Grandma and Grandpa Paradies,' Bo says.

'Yeah,' I say.

When we get to Rotterdam, we keep our mouths shut. Bo knows about the war and the bombardment. That's why we leave Rotterdam alone – it wouldn't be right to wipe out the city all over again. The train stops at Rotterdam Central. Passes through Blaak station. Then we rattle over the old Hef Bridge. The river is as slate-grey and busy as ever. The view of the glittering water summons up deep longings, for distant shores, unfamiliar cities. We like Rotterdam, Bo and I. Sometimes we even go to Feyenoord's home games. (A few years after this, the railway tunnel under the Meuse was opened. The most beautiful stretch of track in the Netherlands became a useless hunk of rust. At Feyenoord, a former Ajax player was appointed trainer. The old stadium had never seen such half-baked football.)

Right before we get to Dordrecht, we send a huge shipyard to the bottom of the Merwede.

'Took care of that one.'

We plough under a tract full of miserable twigs trying to pass for fruit trees, without so much as a by-your-leave. We replace them with standard trees: Triomphe de Vienne, a peach of a pear that's almost disappeared from the Netherlands, because it bruises too easily, and also because it ripens just when the supply of pears is at its peak, and therefore when prices are at their lowest.

At the Biesbosch wetlands we let the tidal waters flow back in, so that the woods make way for reeds again.

'Too bad for the beavers.'

'A real pity.'

A fisherman checks his fish wheel and pulls a salmon out of the net.

'How can you know where you want to go,' I say to Bo, 'if you don't know where we came from?'

And Bo presses his nose against the window and blows up the refinery at Moerdijk. A chip off the old block, I think proudly – I thought proudly.

22

The story of the letter is an old one I borrowed from Monika. A historical event processed into a crock of lies, sort of like the Gulf War.

When I (Monika) was eight, I wrote a letter to my mother. I was at home alone with my mother a lot, because my father worked in a city far from us and came home late at night. I'm an only child. When I was alone with my mother, she ignored me as much as she could. She preferred it when I read a book or played quietly in a corner, as long as I didn't make any noise and didn't bother her by asking questions or telling stories about what had happened at school.

Nothing much ever happened at school, though, and I'd learned a long time ago not to ask my mother questions. She never understood what I meant, or else she didn't understand that I didn't already know the answer to my own question. Whatever it was, she never gave me a normal answer. So I saved all my questions for a friend at school, who then asked his mother, or who sometimes even knew the answer himself, which made him very proud and made me proud too, because it meant our friendship was that much closer.

Seeing as I was never allowed to ask my mother

anything, I decided one day to write her a letter. That wasn't easy, because in a letter you have to write the truth very carefully. If the person you're writing to doesn't understand what you mean, terrible misunderstandings can arise – that much I realized even then. So I took a long time writing the letter. Every day it became a little longer. Every day there were more things about which I thought: I want my mother to know that, to know what I think about that. The letter also contained more and more about what I thought of her and of my father. I remember reading some of those sentences ten times over, to be absolutely sure they said exactly what I meant.

One day I decided the letter was finished. I wrote, 'This is what I wanted to say.' And I signed my name at the bottom.

It was time to give the letter to my mother, but I didn't dare. At first I kept it in my school notebook. But my parents sometimes checked my homework unexpectedly, so that wasn't a safe place. I decided that the best place to hide it was in the attic. I used to play in the attic a lot, with a chest full of old clothes. Above that chest was a place where two rafters crossed. Between the rafters was a little crack. I hid the letter in there. And then, the way kids do, I forgot all about it.

That was the story Monika told, and the story I'm now telling Anke Neerinckx, the wife of my son's father – for there's no longer any doubt in my mind that he's the one who impregnated Monika. *Bo!* keeps hammering away in my head. *Bo!* What a nerve!

*   *   *

'Two weeks ago,' I tell Anke, 'my mother died. And suddenly I remembered that letter. It's become very important for me to know what was in it. To know the way I saw her.'

'You never completely get away from them, do you?' she says. 'Your parents.'

You can hear a pin drop. Outside a car tears through the puddles. The tyres hiss. It sounds as though the rain has eased up.

'Have some more coffee,' Anke says. 'Or would you like something stronger? To get rid of the chill? It would be a good excuse for me to have a drink too. I never drink when I'm home alone.'

'Are you alone often?' I ask, and regret it immediately. 'Excuse me,' I say quickly. 'I didn't mean it that way.'

She laughs. 'Pretty often. Niko, my husband, spends a lot of time abroad. He's a cameraman and director. He has his own video-production company. I have red wine, white, beer, whisky, cognac, Blue Curaçao, young Dutch gin and Baileys.'

'Were you going to open a bottle of wine?'

'I'd love to. Preferably red.'

'Sounds good. I'll join you.'

She brings the bottle of wine into the living room. Takes two glasses from an antique cabinet.

'Niko brought this cabinet back from Sri Lanka. One day there was suddenly a whole container full of colonial furniture on the quay at Rotterdam.'

She asks if I know anything about wine, and shows me the bottle. A Corbières.

'Nothing special, is it?' she asks.

'No, nothing special, but a good wine. A slightly acid aftertaste, with just a hint of soil.'

'Bleccch,' she shudders.

'I'm talking through my hat. I don't know anything about wine.' (For a moment there I consider telling her about my father's wine collection. But I'm afraid of making mistakes, afraid I'll contradict myself if I talk too much about myself. So I don't.)

She uncorks the bottle and fills two glasses.

'Bo, Sam and . . . ?'

'Pim,' she says.

'Nice names.'

'Thank you. They're nice children.'

'Bo,' I say. 'Did your husband have a special reason for naming him Bo?'

'I think he knew a little boy by that name. I'm not really sure. He just thought it was a nice name, he said. Nice and short. Some people think you spell it B-e-a-u, but it's just plain Bo: B-o.'

Monika's parents were very upset about the name we'd chosen. 'Bo?' her mother said on the phone. (Monika was still in bed, recovering, and had made it clear with a look that she didn't want to talk to her mother.) 'How do you spell that? B-e-a-u?'

'No, just plain Bo: B-o,' I said.

'Bo.' The way she pronounced it made it sound like *Boh*.

'Boo!' I said.

'What?'

'Boo! Just kidding.'

'Could I speak to Monika?'

'She's asleep.'

'You're lying, and I know you're lying, but that's just your nature. I can only hope that Boh won't take after his father.' And then, as if shocked by her own nastiness at this joyous moment, she added, 'Well, you know we don't keep up with the times, not like the two of you. I'm sure you two know what's best, don't you?'

The greatest injustice in the whole history of Bo and my infertility is that it wasn't Monika's parents who actually lost their only grandchild, it was my father. Never for a moment have I considered telling him about it – it would break his heart. (Since my mother died, his heart can't take much. He still works every day in the shed behind their house – which has now become *his* house, a fact he hates. He fixes up old furniture, which he then donates to rest homes or the Salvation Army. Sometimes I think it's his way of trying to win himself a place in heaven, or in one of those rest homes. But I don't tell him that. In the evening he drinks a glass of red wine and reads a book, or watches a football match on TV. When I visit him with Ellen and Bo, he perks up completely. That makes me sad.)

In the last few weeks I've often thought: if Monika's parents were the ones whose blood ties with Bo had been so abruptly severed, I would have been *more* than pleased to tell them. I would have hopped into the car, wearing my best suit, and I would have rung their doorbell with a broad grin on my face. And if they didn't open the door, I would have painted the news in huge letters on the street: 'BO ISN'T YOUR GRANDCHILD! HA HA HA!'

But how could Bo not be their grandchild?

Maybe that's the biggest difference between motherly love and fatherly love: a mother is always a hundred per cent certain that her child is truly her child. A mother, therefore, never has to prove herself.

'Where was that crack between the rafters, exactly?'

Her voice makes me jump, as though she's submitting me to an interrogation. But when I look at her she's wearing that friendly smile again, the smile that makes her so attractive. She's a 'pleaser', I think to myself. As are so many beautiful women – her kind of beautiful women.

'To tell you the truth, I don't remember,' I say. 'I mean, I can still see the crack, but not exactly where it was in the attic. Where it was in relation to the steps, for example.'

I have no idea what kind of steps I'm talking about. Do they have a trapdoor with a pull-down ladder, or a real set of stairs? Is there a skylight? No, at least not on the side facing the street.

'There's a trapdoor, with one of those ladders, on the left side of the attic. Against that wall, as it were.' She points to one corner of the living room.

'Well, at least that hasn't changed.'

We sip our wine in silence. And just when I'm thinking that it's time to go (after all, I'll be coming back, and I must pick my way carefully now, I want to see Bo – the

other Bo!), she pushes herself up off the couch and says,
'We took pictures before we renovated the place. Maybe
you'll recognize it then.'

She goes over to another antique colonial cabinet and
comes back with a photo album. She opens the album in
front of me on the glass coffee table (the mahogany base
undoubtedly came from that same container on the quay
at Rotterdam) and kneels down beside it. When I lean
forward to look at the pictures, I can smell her perfume.
Cacharel. Monika hated it. 'Sickly sweet', she called it.
But I always thought it smelled good. I still do.

Anke Neerinckx turns the pages of the photo album
with her neatly manicured hands. I see a man wearing
paint-splotched overalls. Niko? I wouldn't have recognized him. A child playing among piles of planks in a
muddy garden. Bo?

'Here,' she says, and slides the book over a bit so that
I can get a better look. 'I bet you'll recognize this. We
found it when we steamed off the old paper.' I see a
wall with grey-and-green-striped wallpaper. Never have
I seen anything so ugly.

'I'll be damned,' I say. 'How about that?' And I
laugh a little sheepishly. 'My father had terrible taste.
My mother did, too, come to think of it. God rest
her soul.'

'It was a lot of work,' Anke says. A lock of her dark
hair, which she has fastened up with an exotic hairpin
(Sri Lanka?), has fallen loose. The tips of it brush against
her cheek. She tries to push the lock away, but it falls
back again. It's a beautiful gesture, precisely because it's
so futile.

She shows me two more photos of rooms I've never seen before, but I nod in confirmation.

'That's right, that's how it was. I'd forgotten, but now I'd recognize it anywhere. That's how our house looked.'

And then it happens.

She turns a page. A photo slips out. The photo falls to the floor, face down. She picks it up. Turns back the page. There's a white, empty square where the photo had been. She puts the picture back in place, slides the corners into the little paper triangles and closes the book. It all takes no more than a few seconds.

When we've said goodbye at the door (she holds out her hand, and I'm so dazed I almost forget to shake it: 'Ring tomorrow, and we'll arrange a time.'), when I'm down the street and around the corner, when I know for sure that I'm out of earshot, then I scream, '*Monikaaa!*'

I start running. I run straight through puddles, straight through traffic, straight through a crowd hanging around in front of the door of a disco or a mosque or a theatre, I have no idea, I run until I'm completely out of breath, and then I run some more.

It's true.

Niko Neerinckx is the father of my son.

Why else would he keep a picture of Monika in the family album?

23

Facts. Figures. Titbits of information. There are people who know everything there is to know about expensive cars. In which year did what model appear on the market? How big was the engine? How many cylinders did it have? And how much did one pay for the optional gazelle-skin upholstery? For years Bo and I didn't own a car; we only bought one again after Ellen moved in with us. In the meantime, however, we collected a wealth of useless information about old and exclusive cars. We still can't tell a Hyundai from a Toyota, but ask Bo or me about the models of Morris Minor that appeared over the years and you'll receive a detailed reply. That which one doesn't have, but would like to, is what one wishes to know all about. These days I, for example, know everything there is to know about sperm. And about virility and masculine (and feminine) fertility. Facts. Figures. Titbits of information.

On a worldwide average, one out of every ten children is not sired by the man generally assumed to be its father. This figure applies in equal measure to the industrialized West.

A healthy adult male of about thirty who goes to bed

twice a week with the same partner produces 300 million sperm cells every time he has an orgasm. But if he has a fling with a woman he knows already has a partner, he will leave behind twice as many sperm cells: more than 600 million.

In an ejaculation containing 600 million spermatozoids, only 1 million are capable of fertilizing an egg cell. The other reckless swimmers are killer spermatozoids (500 million) and 'blockers'.

Every ejaculation is a declaration of war. Like an army, the killer spermatozoids comb the surroundings in search of enemies. When they encounter such an enemy (a sperm cell belonging to another male, which they recognize by its chemical structure), they release a toxic acid that damages the cell wall of their rival, causing it to burst and die. Meanwhile, the blocker sperm cells move to the narrow passageways of the intrauterine membrane, to prevent the advance of any enemy cells in the direction of the coveted goal (the egg cell). War, in other words, really *is* in our genes.

The longer a man goes without having sexual intercourse with his partner, the more sperm cells he will fire off when the time finally arrives. The reason: the longer he has failed to satisfy his spouse sexually, the greater the chance that she's been unfaithful to him, and therefore the larger the army he will need in order to defeat an enemy. This does not, by the way, apply to situations in which he has never lost sight of the woman in question. The chance that she has been unfaithful to him is then practically nil, and he can make do with a maintenance dosage of 100 to 300 million spermatozoids.

According to a recent British study, 4 per cent of the population is the product of an active, full-blown spermatic war. In other words, one out of every twenty-five conceptions takes place while the womb of the woman in question contains at least two armies of rival spermatozoids. Love is, in more senses than one, a battlefield.

If the statisticians of modern sexological research are right, the spermatic army of Bo's biological father (the army of Niko Neerinckx!) achieved the easiest victory in the history of warfare. Even the Gulf War, in which the ground offensive was decided within thirty-six hours, was a hard-fought victory compared with the walk-over of Neerinckx's troops. Monika's battlefield had the feel of enemy presence; there were even trucks that should have brought in the troops, but there were no soldiers. Not one.

24

Dees is aghast.

'So what now?'

'Yeah, that's what I've been wondering the whole time. What now?'

'When's he coming back?'

'Ten days.'

'Who would ever have thought, a little detective work and bingo, there's the culprit. Niko . . . what's his name again?'

'Neerinckx. With c-k-x.'

'Well, isn't that frightfully la-di-da! Niko Neerinckx. *Bo* Neerinckx. My God, what a mess. Whisky?'

The next day, as agreed, I'd called her – the woman with the pinned-up hair and the sweatpants, the woman who needed company in order to have a drink, the wife of the man who is the father of Bo, of two Bos, in fact. Anke Neerinckx.

'Would this afternoon be convenient?' she asked.

It would.

This time she was wearing black jeans and a man's white shirt that looked good on her, the way almost anything would have looked good on her. She showed me to the attic. On the way up the stairs I looked at her arse (it was dancing right in front of my face – nice, tight buttocks). She pulled the trapdoor, and the ladder slid down with dry little clicks.

'After you,' she said.

The attic was full of the kind of things attics are supposed to be full of. Suitcases and boxes and skis and an old-fashioned armchair. I looked at the rafters. There weren't many cracks. She came up the ladder after me.

'Is it all coming back to you now?'

'No,' I said, speaking truthfully. 'There was a lot more junk then. It was a kind of maze. That's why I liked coming up here. I could pretend I was in a completely different world.' I'd lost none of my capacity for inundating her with lies. I walked around, inspecting the roof, and finally found a crack at a place where two rafters crossed, exactly the way I'd imagined it.

'Damn,' I said. 'Here it is.'

She came and stood close to me. Again I smelled her perfume. I stood on tiptoe and peered into the crack.

'I don't see anything.'

I took a step back, so she could look as well. Her arm brushed mine.

'Nope,' she said. 'But wait a minute.'

She went over to a big steamer trunk close to the trapdoor, opened it and took out a torch. 'Here, try this.'

I took the torch and tried to turn it on. It didn't work.

'Oh yeah, I forgot,' she said, and laughed. I handed her the torch and she unscrewed it, took out the top battery and turned it around. 'One of Niko's things,' she said. 'He always turns a battery around so they won't run down by accident.'

'Handy,' I say.

'No it's not.' She laughed, as if she was saying something naughty. She's flirting, I thought. That's the kind of woman she is, a tease and a flirt. But woe betide the man who draws the wrong conclusions. She handed me the torch and I shone it into the crack. There was nothing there. She came up beside me for another look too. She brought her face up close to mine. I felt that lock of hair, which had fallen free again today, brush my cheek. A shiver ran down my spine.

'What a pity!' she said, and the way she looked at me seemed to express real disappointment. 'Oh, what a pity!' she said again. I was ashamed at making her feel disappointed while I, of course, was feeling nothing – nothing but heady excitement at her being so close. I walked around the attic a bit more, as if in doubt about the exact location. Maybe I'd hidden the letter somewhere else? But there were no other cracks.

'I used to be afraid of attics,' she said suddenly.

'Why?'

'I was afraid strange men were hiding in them. And now look at me . . . up in my own attic with a strange man.'

'I'm completely harmless.'

'One can never be sure.'

We went down the ladder again, first me, then her, so I looked at her buttocks again, dancing down this time.

'Would you like to see the kids' rooms?' she asked after I had pushed the ladder back up for her and closed the trapdoor. 'Where did you use to sleep?'

'At the back.'

'That's Bo's room now.'

As if I hadn't guessed. She showed me the room. It didn't look at all like the one where my own Bo (my *own* Bo?!) slept. Bo didn't get a room of his own until he turned four. Shortly after Monika's death I was offered another house, through one of my father's real-estate contacts. 'It isn't good for you to stay here,' my father had said. I think my parents knew I was drowning my sorrows in bars. But they never said a thing about it. They kept asking me how I was getting on, though, and they invited me over for dinner all the time, or 'for a decent glass of wine', as my father put it. I didn't take them up on it much. I still don't know why, but I think it had something to do with shame. I felt like a failure. My father and mother had been together so long, and even though they may not have made each other really happy any more, at least they didn't make each other *un*happy. And what about me? What had I accomplished? Monika and I had been together for barely five years. Her death wasn't my fault, of course, not as her parents wanted me to believe, but still . . . If I'd called the doctor a little sooner, would she still be alive? I've buried that thought, but I can't dispose of it completely. The feeling of being my father's equal, the feeling I'd had when Monika became pregnant, had died along with her. I'd been demoted. I was a son again. It hurt me to disappoint my mother, but I couldn't find the right words to explain to her what was going on inside me.

Bo's room in our new house wasn't very big, not much bigger than the room of this other Bo, the one I was standing in now. But two rooms could hardly have been more different. Here there was fire-engine-red linoleum on the floor, while my Bo (*my* Bo?) had sisal mat. Here was a bed with an Ajax bedspread, and the canary-yellow wall opposite the window bore a big poster of Bert and Ernie. Bo had a mattress on the floor, at his own insistence. ('The world is nicest closer to the ground,' he'd said.) The bedspread was a patchwork quilt my mother had made for him. On the walls of Bo's room were dozens of pictures of exotic animals, clipped from the pages of *National Geographic*. Gruesome spiders with hairy legs, a manatee with her calf, a kangaroo rat, a flying fox, a lot of lizards. His room hasn't changed much since then. The quilt has been replaced by a South American blanket Ellen brought home from one of her trips. (Bo's mice had pissed on the quilt, and the guinea pig had gnawed holes in it.) Once Bo had outgrown the mice and guinea-pig phase, the lizards on the wall were finally joined by real lizards in a terrarium. When he was ten he'd replaced the pictures on the walls with a series of dinosaur posters. Those posters are still there. And beside the terrarium there's now a collection of glass jars and plastic containers in which he raises insects, as lizard feed and objects of study. Of all the toys I saw in the room of *this* Bo, the Bo of Niko and Anke Neerinckx, there was nothing my Bo had ever played with.

'He must be a cheerful kid,' I said, just to have something to say.

'He gets that from me,' she said, 'not from his father.'

The other bedroom was a copy of Bo's, except the fire-engine red and canary yellow had made way for cobalt blue and apple green. And instead of one bed, there were two. Each with an Ajax bedspread.

'I didn't want Sam to have a girl's room,' she said. 'And Pim likes sleeping in the same room as his sister. Better than with Bo, because he's still the littlest. This way he can still play big brother.' Her babbling about the children like that gave our being there together something almost improperly intimate. But the bedroom she shared with Niko remained closed to me. And I couldn't come up with a ready excuse for wanting to see it.

'Do you have children of your own?' she asked, once we were back downstairs.

'No,' I said. And I thought: you're lying the truth.

'I'm going to tell you something you might not like to hear.'

Dees has been quiet for a while, during which time he's polished off two glasses of whisky. I'd been sitting there thinking about Anke Neerinckx and the pictures she'd shown me (giving her yet another excuse to have a glass of wine; at two in the afternoon, no less).

'I think,' Dees says, 'you'd be better off not confronting him with this. Wait, wait, wait a minute! I said you might not like what I have to say, but I'm your best friend. At least give me a chance to finish.'

I lean back in my chair and fold my arms across my chest.

'The Unwilling Ear,' says Dees. 'That's what they should call that pose of yours. But try to imagine, Armin, what will happen when you tell him what you've found out.' (When Dees calls me Armin, things have become serious.)

'To start with, he could claim paternity.'

'Why would he do that, after all these years?'

'Because his own marriage hits the rocks, for example. How do you think this Anke is going to react when she finds out he named their oldest son after a child he had by another woman? I don't think she'll take that lightly. So he'll think you've ruined his marriage. And the only way he can still get something out of having sired that kid is to claim paternity.'

'It would never hold up in court.'

'Well, first of all, I'm not so sure. But even more important: do you *want* to go to court? Do you want to do that to yourself? And to Bo? And to Ellen?'

I take a sip of whisky. There's a lot of truth in what he's saying. It *would* be much smarter just to let things lie.

'But I need answers, Dees,' I say. 'I want to know how and why and when and where and a lot more.'

'Is that what you really want? Is it going to help you to know how Monika undressed for him? Do you really want to know if she had an orgasm? Or whether it happened at your place or at his, or on a table covered with colourful holiday brochures from that drippy travel agency? Is it going to do you any good to know whether he got excited by that scar on her stomach? All I'm trying to say, Armin, is that if you talk to him, if you interrogate him, you have no control over what you're going to find out – or not find out. Remember those stories Robbert tried to put over on you? The answers you get could very well be harder to live with than the questions. That's all I wanted to say. Could we have two more of the same?'

*   *   *

Honesty is the basis of all friendship, but it can also destroy a friendship. Or a love.

Anke Neerinckx had shown me a picture of her oldest son.

'How old would he be in this picture?'

'Five.'

The five-year-old Bo is sitting on a plastic tractor. The tractor is next to a garden fence. The little boy is staring across the fence, into the wide world. There's a great longing in his eyes.

'Small as he is,' the proud mother says, 'he's already a real man. Dreaming of great adventures.'

'Don't women dream of adventure?'

'Sure. But they're not like men; they look for it closer to home.'

'"Living on the edge at home".'

'That's right.'

And her eyes meet mine. And our bodies touch, albeit ever so slightly. On the couch, with the photo album between us, on her lap and a little bit on mine.

Ellen once called me a 'non-threatening male'. 'That's why women confide in you so easily,' she said. I never could decide whether I was pleased by that, but for the first time in years I'm overtaken by the lust to violate that confidence in a terrible way. But I don't do it. I don't even move. I look at the picture of the boy on his tractor. And the moment passes and she turns the page and together we look at a picture of her and Niko, laughing as they paint a wall.

Life is an endless string of remodellings.

25

On the morning of Bo's eighth birthday, I got out of bed at five. I turned on the light in the kitchen, put the kettle on to boil, took a shower. Hair still wet, I fried eggs and bacon, filled a big thermos flask with coffee and a smaller one with tea. I stared at my reflection in the window while the butter spattered in the pan. 'You're turning into an old prune face,' I said to myself. Then I went in and woke Bo.

'Bo! Bo! Happy birthday!'

We ate our breakfast of crunchy oatmeal and fruit without a word, and while Bo was getting dressed I made bacon and egg sandwiches, with mayonnaise instead of butter, and with plenty of salt, exactly the way he likes it.

Bo didn't really wake up until we were in the car.

'Where's my present? Don't I get a present?'

'We're going fishing. Isn't that a present?'

In my five years with Monika, I never went fishing. It was the only real sacrifice I had to make for her. She would never have forgiven me otherwise. 'Driving a hook through the mouth of a living animal, just for the fun of it,' Monika said when she discovered my rods in a corner of my room. 'I think that's about as low as a human being can get.'

'Is it cause enough to reconsider?' I asked. She'd just confessed to Robbert that there was another man in her life. (Her words, not mine – when it came to love, Monika adored high-flown texts. Monika never said 'fucking': she said 'making love' or 'sleeping with someone'. While in my view, what she did, what *we* did, was what you really call fucking.)

'It *should* give me cause to reconsider,' she said. 'But I'm afraid that this time the spirit is once again weaker than the flesh.'

'Would it help if I promised never to fish again as long as you're in my life?'

'That would be a great help,' Monika said. That's how it happened. I only went fishing again when Bo turned five, and then only because he wanted to so badly. My own feeling about it was that it wouldn't be fair to Monika to start torturing innocent fish again, simply because she'd had the misfortune to die young. That death had caused enough suffering, without adding to it the suffering of fish. (Fishing is, of course, a form of cruelty to animals – but it's such a *beautiful* form, almost as beautiful as bullfighting, for which I have a secret soft spot.)

When I'd told him that going fishing was a present, too, Bo had looked at me doubtingly. But I simply kept my eyes on the road, which was misty and still largely shrouded in darkness, and said nothing. By the time we got to the boat-hire place, the eastern sky was dark violet. Hesitantly, the land took on its first colour.

'Your rod!' I shouted when I opened the trunk. 'We forgot your fishing rod!'

Bo didn't say a thing.

'I guess we'll just have to take turns with mine.'

Bo stared at the ground.

'Come on.'

He dragged his feet, but not for long.

'Hey,' I said after the man from the hirer's had taken us to our boat. 'What's that?' Lying on the bottom of the boat there was a long dark-green object with a yellow ribbon around it.

'My present!' Bo shouted in amazement.

And so we rowed out onto the lake. The shores were deserted and we fished in silence, and only a moorhen saw us and was startled and withdrew into the reeds. Bo's little hand clenched his new fishing rod. His knuckles were white. Occasionally our floats dipped out of sight. Occasionally the water churned and splashed.

At nine o'clock I rowed the boat over to the shore, where a coffee house had just opened its doors for business. There I phoned Bo's school.

'My son is sick.'

'Nothing serious, I hope.'

'No, nothing serious.'

'That's a relief. Be sure to wish him a happy birthday, would you?'

By the end of the day we had caught eleven roach, four white bream, six bream and a mirror carp. Bo caught the mirror carp. It was his first, and a miracle his line held. When the fish was lying on the bottom of the boat, gasping for air with its big rubbery mouth, I leaned over and sniffed.

'What do you smell?' Bo asked.

'Try it.'

He leaned over the fish and sniffed.

'I smell fish.'

'And the wondrous odour of the underwater world,'
I said.

He sniffed again, then nodded. 'Yeah,' he said. 'The
wondrous odour of the underwater world.'

Next week Bo is going to turn fourteen. For the first
time, I have no idea what to give him.

26

'Light and darkness, life and death, right and left, are brothers of one another,' the apostle Philip wrote. 'They are inseparable. Because of this neither are the good good, nor the evil evil, nor is life life, nor death death.'

Monika cheated on Robbert P. F. Hubeek with me. Monika cheated on me with Niko Neerinckx. I cheated on Monika with Ellen. Ellen cheated on Monika with me.

But only once.

It happened six months after the night Monika told us she was pregnant. One cold Saturday evening in January I went into town alone. During the last few days Monika had been tired and irritable. She was lying on the couch with a blanket over her, watching TV, her stomach bulging up beneath the tartan rug.

'Bye,' I said, and kissed her on the forehead.

'Have fun.'

The sky was clear and the trees in the park stood motionless in the quiet winter evening. The first layers of ice were forming along the edges of the pond. A duck quacked. I decided not to take my bike, but to walk into town. The city can be my greatest enemy (when the streets clog up with cars and couriers on scooters, with testy pedestrians and cyclists concerned only with their own survival), but also my best friend. That evening the city helped me shake off the uneasiness that I'd been dragging along behind me for a few days and that hung in the house on the Ceintuurbaan like stale cigarette smoke.

At Café de Kerk I drank two beers and listened to a muddled conversation between an old actor and a tatty woman with a tiny little Yorkshire terrier in her handbag that began peeping nervously every time the actor raised his voice.

'We spin the threads of our own lives, but God weaves the carpet.'

De Kerk was the ideal spot to start off a night of cheerful drinking. Or to end one.

At Muntplein I saw a boy throw a milkshake at a passing tram. The pink shake splattered and left a freakish spot on the window. A passenger stuck up his middle finger.

I followed the narrow pavement that separates the street from the waters of the Rokin. Another duck quacked. Without birds the city would be absolutely uninhabitable. As always, Queen Wilhelmina was sitting frozen on her horse. She looked as though she could have done with the heavy overcoat she wore in another statue, on the other side of town, in the square that bears her name.

At Zeppo's, in an alleyway called Prayer With No End, I had two more beers and looked at the students and congratulated myself for the umpteenth time on the fact that Monika and I had turned our backs on the university for good. All that bourgeois chichi was painful to behold. I had the urge to get right up the noses of a couple of those gold-spectacled, pin-striped kids. (Not long before that, I'd told Monika's father that there were very few things I considered unforgivable, but that being intelligent and still a right-winger was definitely one of them. A statement, her father said, which merely demonstrated my own shocking lack of intelligence, and their own daughter's lack of sound judgement.) But I held myself in check this time, paid up and went on my way. The night was still young. Why should I waste my time on boys who got excited about stock-market reports, or girls who thought a sweater was meant for tying around your neck, rather than putting on (or taking off)?

I decided to go to De String, on the Nes, to catch some live music until it was late enough to go to the disco. Monika and I may have been on the verge of becoming parents, but we'd promised each other we'd never turn into buttoned-down homebodies. And that evening I meant to make good on our promise. To drink a little, dance a little, flirt a little, and finally, tired and drunk but content, to stagger home and crawl in beside that warm, pregnant body. That's what I would do – and that's what I would have done had I not run into Ellen at De String.

She blushed when she saw me. ('You blushed when you saw me,' Ellen would say later.) We'd seen each other only once since that wonderful night, and that had been in Monika's company, in which company we both felt at home and in which what we felt for each other (whatever that was) was as plain and natural as what we felt for her. Like that very first time, Ellen was tanned, a beacon of health in a sea of Dutch drabness.

A quartet was playing Irish drunkards' tunes and ballads full of maritime romance and emigrant suffering. I ordered a Jameson's, with one ice cube. Ellen was drinking red wine.

'So how are you doing?'

'Good.'

'Are you here by yourself?'

'Yeah. You too, by the looks of it.'

'Monika's too pregnant to roam around on Saturday night. Have you just got back from somewhere?'

'Ecuador.'

'Don't tell me, not with that . . . What's his name again?'

'Niko. No, I was there with a group. Exhausting. But fun. And less frustrating than with someone you're in love with but who doesn't even know you exist.'

A couple at a little table in the corner got up to leave, and Ellen and I edged our way through the crowd to grab their seats. For a while we listened to the music without talking. Then Ellen tugged on my sleeve, and I leaned over to her so she wouldn't have to shout above the music. With her mouth close to my ear, she said, 'Had you ever gone to bed with two women at the same time before?'

I laughed and shook my head. 'What about you? I mean . . .'

'No.'

We stopped talking for a while, but when I glanced

over at her again I saw a smile on her lips. She turned to me and looked me straight in the eye, and the smile grew broader.

'That kind of thing only happens when Monika's around,' she said.

And I nodded and thought: it's not over yet.

(There's always a convenient excuse for adultery. According to the most recent sociobiological insights, the urge to commit adultery is genetically embedded in both men and women: adultery – so long as it remains undiscovered – increases reproductive success.)

We stayed for the end of the set. Then I suggested we go somewhere else. Outside, Ellen put her arm through mine and led me to a café I'd never been to before. Not too crowded, but not too quiet, either. When we went in they were playing something by the Velvet Underground, and for the rest of the evening the old hits just kept on coming, by Dr Hook and the Medicine Show and Credence Clearwater Revival and the Rolling Stones. The clientele seemed to be a carefully selected cross-section of Amsterdam nightlife, which brought with it an extremely atypical camaraderie (not a single subculture was dominant enough to impose its own code of behaviour on anyone else). We settled down at a table on a dais at the back of the café, and Ellen ordered a bottle of red wine and two glasses – another of the place's unique features: you could order wine by the bottle, and for twenty guilders you got a more than reasonable Rioja instead of the kind of sourish

Corbières or a Côtes-du-Rhône that cost four guilders and seventy-five cents in the supermarket.

'To the new life,' Ellen said.

'To the new life.'

'What are the two most important things you'd like to pass along to your child?' she asked.

I had to think about that one. I rarely thought about fatherhood in such concrete terms.

'Love, and a deep suspicion of public opinion,' I said then.

'Which spot in Holland are you most looking forward to showing your child?'

'The Wadden Shallows at low tide, in autumn, when a peregrine is hunting and the sun is literally blocked out by a cloud of stilts.'

'What piece of music would you like it to hear?'

'Bach's *St Matthew Passion*.'

'That's so sorrowful!'

'But also comforting. And everything Dolly Parton ever did, of course.'

'What's your earliest memory?'

'Is this an interrogation?'

'Yes.'

'Dressing up like a princess. We had a big wicker basket full of old clothes. My mother's wedding veil was in there, too. I put it on. I can't remember what else I had on. But I remember standing in front of the mirror and finding myself beautiful and very charming. My mother says I was three at the time.'

'Who was your first real love?'

'Jacqueline van Essen. At junior school. A little girl

with glasses and a round face with chubby cheeks, sort of like Queen Beatrix in her early photos. She called me the apple of her eye. I thought a lot about that expression: apple, eye, apple of my eye. Nice expression. Mysterious. Why would you call someone the apple of your eye? But I was very flattered. And I fell in love right away. Must have lasted at least six months, which is an eternity at that age.'

We sat and talked like that until the wine was finished. Then I drank a beer and Ellen had a Spa, with bubbles.

When we were back outside, I said: 'I'll walk you home.' ('She lives on Love Street, lingers long on Love Street,' Jim Morrison was singing inside.)

'But it's out of your way.'

'Monika would never forgive me if I let her best friend walk home alone in the middle of the night.'

It wasn't far to Ellen's house. She lived at the edge of the Jordaan. And of course she asked me to come up and get warm (the temperature by then had dropped well below freezing, an east wind had come up and cut right through my jacket and, besides, it wasn't the kind of evening one concludes by saying goodbye on a windy pavement.) Her house was small and soberly furnished. Wooden floors with here and there a carpet or a throw rug from Asia or Latin America. A single bookcase full of travel guides. A wooden Buddha on the mantelpiece. A poster of a Guatemalan Indian on the wall. She put the kettle on in the tiny kitchen, then came and sat beside me on the sofa. And before the tea had even drawn, we were lying on the floor and my hands were gliding over her breasts and she was blowing softly in my ear.

Everything was familiar, and everything was new.

We went to her bedroom. She took the teapot and two cups with her. She lit two candles. We undressed and crawled into her bed, which was cold but soon warmed up. We kissed and caressed and she said, 'Just once. No more than that.'

And I said, 'Yeah, one time.' And we looked at each other when I went into her and we said again, 'Just once.'

Afterwards we drank our tea, close together, with the duvet pulled as high as it would go. And I said, 'It wasn't over yet.'

And she said, 'No.'

But suddenly our voices sounded different. Suddenly we weren't so sure of ourselves any more. When I'd finished my tea, I dressed quickly and kissed her goodbye.

'Be careful' was the last thing she said.

(The desire to keep adultery secret is also genetically determined, says the sociobiologist. Discovery increases the chance of violence and abandonment, and therefore reduces the progeny's chance of survival. But, according to Dees, sociobiologists suffer from a chronic lack of knowledge of molecular biology, and so their theories are built on shifting sand.)

27

'Bookkeepers is what they are,' says Dees. 'And not very creative ones at that.'

We're on our third glass of cognac. After Dees's wise words about living with questions and living with answers, the subject of 'Bo's biological father' (meanwhile narrowed down to 'Niko Neerinckx') had never been touched on again. By way of the melting of the polar icecaps and the recruitment policy at Feyenoord Football Club, we've arrived quite naturally at one of Dees's hobbyhorses. He says, 'They run the bookkeeping for a bankrupt world-view, the way the accountants of the Third Reich kept careful track of how much Zyklon-B was being used, while the Allied bombers had already blasted half the country to rubble and the Russians were marching into Berlin.'

Whenever Dees gets wound up, he starts talking about the war. He got that from his father. 'It's in my genes,' he actually admits, even though he, of all people, knows what nonsense that is. The biggest popular lie of our day is that everything is in our genes – says Dees.

'These so-called modern biologists have a number of preconceptions about how the world is organized, and anything that supports those preconceptions is broken down and studied until the cows come home. All they do is bend over backwards to verify their own reductionist-mechanist world-view. Every once in a great while, of course, some smart alec comes along and proposes research that might undermine that world-view. What am I saying? Every once in a great while some madman actually starts that kind of research and writes an article about it!'

He takes another slug of his cognac.

'Articles like that do not find a place in our publication. We will tolerate no muttering in the ranks.'

There's no better remedy for depression, despair, melancholy and that run-down, helpless feeling than an evening out, chewing the fat with Dees about the state of the world in general and science in particular. For years, Dees has been working on a book that will disprove Darwin's theory of evolution once and for all.

'Microbiology will deliver Darwin the *coup de grâce*, just you wait!' It's the same thing he'd said back when he banished me from the publishing house, because he felt I should be dealing with losing Monika, even though he never said that in so many words. For a while we saw each other only in bars, where I was to be found even more often than he was – and that's saying something. Sometimes I would leave Bo at my parents' house. They let him sleep in my old room, in my old bed, the bed where Monika and I had once fucked. (That was while my parents were on holiday. We were taking care of the post and watering the plants. It made us feel like naughty children. When we were finished, Monika said, 'What were your adolescent fantasies?' When I told her, she laughed so hard that she peed in my bed. But my parents never found out, and fortunately Bo didn't, either.)

But I usually took Bo along to the bar. He slept well there, although no one noticed; he'd stopped closing his eyes by then. Bo never had nightmares in bars, though. He would drink big glasses of milk, or apple juice from the bottle. And he thought it smelled nice. 'It stinks really nice here,' he said on his first visit. No one ever talked about passive smoking in those days – PC puritanism hadn't been invented yet.

'In Darwin's day,' said Dees, 'they had no idea what the inside of a cell looked like. That's why he could claim that the eye had evolved from photosensitive cells. What did he know about what went on inside a photosensitive cell – let alone *how* it went on? He didn't have the faintest about all the things that have to happen in order to bring about the simplest functional change in a cell like that, to say nothing of a structural *improvement*. Darwin had no way of knowing that cells are full of irreducibly complex systems – and systems like that are fatal for evolutionary theory.'

(Irreducibly complex systems, as Dees has explained to me many times since, cannot be created step by step, by means of minor, random genetic mutations. They work as a mousetrap, for example, does: only when all the parts are in the right place and serve the right function at the right moment. If one single part is absent, or if it doesn't do what it's supposed to do, the whole system fails – and therefore constitutes a useless adaptation, which will disappear under the pressure of natural selection.)

'These days,' Dees went on, 'every molecular biologist knows that the vast majority of systems he studies are irreducibly complex. And therefore that the pillars of all of modern-day biology are rotten to the core. The only thing is, they're afraid to tell anyone. Because then the whole neo-Darwinist house of cards will come crashing down!'

Dees was drinking margaritas at the time, which had something to do with a holiday love affair. I was drinking red wine. The intoxication brought on by red wine makes sorrow both greater and more bearable. I could sit there listening to Dees and, at the same time, my sorrow at Monika's death could be big enough to fill the whole café. Then it was as though the noise, the voices, the music, were coming to me through a wall of cotton wool (only Dees's voice remained the same; every word of his excited argument came across loud and clear, so that years later I could still play it back almost verbatim – to his astonishment). At the same time, it was as though I was no longer sitting opposite him at the table, my three-year-old son on my lap, but floating through space, up through the cigarette smoke and the stench of stale beer, sweaty bodies and cheap perfume, and looking down from on high on the roiling mass, like a bird, a dead soul, like God himself. And all around me my sorrow kept expanding, filling the city, the country, the stratosphere. At moments like that I believed I knew what Bo dreamed of when he fell off the world.

'I'm telling you,' Dees said, 'Hitler's ideas about race were based on better arguments than Darwin's theory of evolution.'

We drank to that, and we ordered another margarita and another carafe of red wine. And I said, 'You hear that, Bo? Don't go looking for things that confirm your pet opinions. Look for things that kick the props out from under them. Thus spoke Uncle Dees.'

But Bo hadn't heard a thing. Bo was sleeping with his eyes wide open. And now, ten years later, I'm sitting with Dees in the bar again, talking once again about wrong-headed theories and world-views that are maintained even though everyone knows better, and I think: man is incapable of learning.

28

Studies have shown that visitors coming to congratulate parents after a birth are much more likely to say that the child resembles its father than its mother. The explanation the researchers give for this is that the visitors are unconsciously trying to put the father's mind at ease.

There are, of course, cases where the baby is the spitting image of its father. The resemblance between George W. Bush and his father is so strong that one wonders whether Mrs Bush was involved in the process at all, or whether one can speak here of the first successful human clone. But if Jordi's last name wasn't Cruyff, who would think he was the son of the greatest football player who ever lived? And who, purely on the basis of appearance, would ever pick Claus von Amsberg as the biological father of Crown Prince Willem-Alexander of Oranje-Nassau? Alex takes after his mother. Like Bo, the eldest son of Niko and Anke Neerinckx. While Bo, the only son of the late Monika Paradies, looks just as much (or as little) like his mother as he does like the man he calls his father, but who isn't.

But does Bo look like Niko Neerinckx? No. At least, not like the photos I've seen of Niko Neerinckx. And not like my memory of him, even if that memory is vague and no doubt unreliable. But does that mean anything?

Can we, on the basis of a lack of resemblance between father and son, draw any conclusions about the love life of Mrs Cruyff or that of the Queen?

For anyone in search of his son's father, physical appearance is an unreliable indicator. A DNA test would probably provide a definite answer, but I'm not sure I dare push things in that direction. As usual, Dees is right: no one can guarantee that it will be easier for me to live with the answers than with the questions. So I am not going to confront Niko Neerinckx with what I've found out.

But I will not give up the chance to dig even further into his private life!

Call it vengefulness or call it perversion, but when Anke and I had searched fruitlessly that afternoon for the imaginary letter in the crack between the rafters, when we'd looked at her photos and she said she had to pick up the children from school, when I stood up and put on my coat and stood at the door and turned to her, she'd given me a look that was both innocent and sly (because it was the look of a young girl in a woman of thirty-five) and said, 'If you're ever in the neighbourhood again, be sure to drop by. I enjoyed it.'

And I said, 'I'll do that.'

The biggest cliché in the mythology of modern sexuality is the lonely housewife who drags the window-cleaner, the plumber or postman into bed. But it could have evolved into such a cliché only, the sexologists assure us, because it reflects daily practice in our sex lives, which are in turn the direct result of our selfish genes.

A man with a good job at an insurance company may offer the stability that is, historically speaking, one of the most important factors for the successful raising of progeny, but otherwise a man like that is probably not a winner. He can't compete physically with outdoor men, with men who earn their livelihood with their bodies and their hands, rather than with their heads (or with overhead projectors, spreadsheets, computer programs, video cameras and monitors).

Window-cleaners, plumbers and postmen are the ideal opponents for a good spermatic war – not least because the chance of discovery is minimal.

So how does Erik Aldenbos, the alter ego with which I have invaded the life and home of Anke Neerinckx, fit into all this? Does Anke Neerinckx want to go to bed with him? Are her genes sending her down the garden path of adultery and deceit, or do they recognize in him, childless after all, an inferior sperm donor, and is she therefore lacking in any lust for him whatsoever?

I'd never realized how pleasant it could be to suddenly have a second identity at one's disposal. To no longer have to be Armin Minderhout, with a dead, adulterous sweetheart, a child not his own and a woman who wants to marry him but whom he can never provide with offspring. Erik Aldenbos is the poor man's alternative to buying a one-way ticket to the far side of the world. (That thought as well, of buying a one-way ticket to the other side of the world, has been raising its head ever since I first heard the words 'Klinefelter's Syndrome'.)

On a sunny spring day, just before noon, Erik Aldenbos

is standing in front of the home of Anke Neerinckx. Under his arm he has a wooden box containing two bottles of an exceptionally fine white Bordeaux: Château Anniche 1992. A firm, fine-dry wine, more floral than fruity, and with a heady bouquet owing to the use of the Sauvignon grape. This time he phoned first. Whether it was convenient. (Whether her husband was at home.) It was convenient. (He was *not* at home.)

She opens the door wearing a pair of light summer trousers and a loose T-shirt. Homey, easy, but at the same time well considered, carefully coordinated. The soft blue of the shirt goes well with the colour of her eyes. She's wearing linen shoes, somewhere between espadrilles and slippers. She is a housewife, but a house-wife of the world. I present her with the box of wine and think: this is a B-movie. B-movies always have a happy ending, but I almost never watch them all the way to the end.

The table is set with black plastic place-mats, rough ceramic plates and a set of sturdy, emphatically designed stainless-steel cutlery. The wine glasses rest on clear blue bases. On the yellow-plastered wall above our heads an old station clock is ticking away.

'Cheers,' she says, once the butter is on the table, and the fresh salmon, and the capers, and the olives, the chorizo and the ciabatta, the little dish of currant jam with the silver spoon her grandmother had left her and, of course, the fresh croissants.

'To the good life.'

'To living on the edge at home.' And we touch glasses and drink and laugh and eat and the sun shines through

the window and above our heads the clock is ticking and
she wants to know who I am, and I am slowly becoming
curious myself, and so I start down the treacherous road
of truth, lies and fabrication that should lead to the
answer to the question: who is Erik Aldenbos, and will
he fuck Anke Neerinckx?

'What do you do for a living?' she asks.

'I'm a freelance editor for a scientific publisher.'

'Married, engaged, divorced, single?'

'Single.'

'Why?'

'Why not?'

'Because it's nicer to be one of two than to be alone.'

'You think so?'

'Don't you?'

'Not necessarily. It depends.'

'On what?'

'On the other person, to start with. I mean, the other
person has to be worth it.'

'Worth what?'

'Everything you have to give up.'

'Do you have a lot to give up?'

'I should be asking you that. Did you have a lot to
give up?'

'Yes,' she says.

'And now you're going to tell me that you get a lot
back in return.'

'That's right.' And she laughs and takes a bite of
her croissant, and a little jam sticks to her upper lip
and after a while she licks it away with the tip of her
tongue and takes a sip of wine and asks, 'Have you

ever loved anyone enough to want to share your life with them?'

'Yes.'

'So what went wrong?'

'She left me for someone else.'

'You know,' she says with sudden fervour, 'when I was eighteen, I knew one thing for sure: I was never going to let myself be reduced to the clichés that all the people around me had been reduced to. And now look at me.'

'How did you meet your husband?'

'On a trip. He was the tour guide. What a cliché.' She laughs mockingly.

'You were with your boyfriend at the time,' I say. 'The two of you were trying to save your relationship by taking a trip together.'

She looks at me in amazement. Then bursts out laughing. 'Yeah, exactly! My God, is it so predictable? Oh, that's terrible!'

'Doesn't matter,' I say. 'When you're eighteen, telling yourself that you're never going to become like all those other stuffy people is just as much a cliché as becoming like them in the end. The things pop stars say about love are just as empty as the marriage of the average teenager's parents – the only difference is that the teenager doesn't know that yet.'

'So what are we supposed to do? I mean, what do we do when we finally work that out? Are we supposed to just give up on love, write it off, put it out with the rubbish?'

'We have to reinvent it,' I say, with no idea what I mean by that.

'What do you mean by that?'

'There's the kind of love our parents have, or at least the image children have, and have always had, of that kind of love. A love based on agreements, on a practical urge to survive. It's a love that young people feel doesn't deserve to be called love. It's a pragmatic love, so at best only a halfway form. And then there's the kind of love young people have: unconditional love, the great, compelling, all-consuming love, the love that's been sung about in a hundred thousand number-one hits. But that's also a halfway form at best, because it's a utopian love. And utopias, once realized, immediately become their opposite. The way great, compelling loves, once they become something lasting, always turn into a hell. Read Pinter. That's why romantic heroes have only one way of surviving: by dying young. If Romeo and Juliet had been given the chance to marry, they would never have found a place in world literature. Or it would have to have been in *Who's Afraid of Virginia Woolf?*'

'So?'

'So what?'

'Well, you said we have to invent love all over again. But how do you do that?'

'The love our parents have and the love experienced by young people have one thing in common,' I say, with no idea what's coming next. 'They're both selfish. Maybe the love we have to reinvent is a love that's no longer self-centred. Maybe love looks completely different from what we suppose. Maybe it doesn't come from us at all. Not from our hearts, as romantics believe, or from our brains, as the rationalists think, or from our genes, as the biologists say. Maybe love is nothing but that which gives life. And you can take part in that, or you can seal yourself off from it. You can help it along, or you can struggle against it. But then again, maybe this is all a bunch of nonsense.'

('God is love,' I'd told Bo when he was still very little, 'and love is God.' But later, after Monika was dead and I'd told him about God's Dark Room in the House of Knowledge, he came back from school one afternoon and said, 'There's a boy in my class who says God is a big beam of light, sort of like the sun but different. And if you do something wrong, he gets angry, and he roars, just like a thunderstorm. Is that true?' And I said, 'No, that's not true.' And he asked, 'So what is it?' And I said, 'We can't know God. God is a mystery that can't be solved.' The same goes for love.)

Did Erik Aldenbos go to bed with Anke Neerinckx?

No.

Could he have?

Yes, says Erik Aldenbos, unhindered by the self-examination that inevitably follows the discovery that your own child isn't yours.

Would the ultimate revenge be to fuck the wife of the man who fucked your wife?

No. The ultimate revenge is *not* to do it, even though you could have. (I tell myself in the train all the way back to Amsterdam. I don't succeed much longer than that.)

29

'Was Niko Neerinckx at the funeral?'

'Oh, Armin, do you still think he's the one who did it?'

'I only asked whether he was at the funeral.'

'Of course he was. Everyone from Small World was there.'

She's right. They were all there. Except for two tour guides who were in Africa at the time. Monika had taken her last trip just before that. Within a few weeks she was going to start a new job.

I was the one who had rung Small World the day Monika died. That afternoon, two of her colleagues were going to come to the hospital. I rang to say it was no longer necessary. All the phone conversations I had in those days are still fresh in my mind. It was as though I had shut out all other impressions and registered only those conversations, with painful precision. What made the greatest impression on me was the silence at the other end, every time I said what had happened.

'You don't have to come to the hospital. Monika passed away this morning.'

Silence.

'She regained consciousness for a moment, yesterday.

She said: "I'm going to die. I'm sorry." And she never woke up again.'

Silence.

'Monika is dead.'

Silence.

'She sighed once. Deeply. Then it was over.'

Silence.

I used different words each time, but each time the reaction was the same. Except with Monika's mother. She hung up right away.

My mother was silent for a long time. Then she starting sobbing quietly. 'Oh, Armin. Oh, Armin, oh, Armin.' Then my father came on the line. 'Tell me it's not true!' 'It's true.' 'Oh God! Oh God! Oh God!'

There was a lot of crying at the other end of the line. But I couldn't cry.

Not even when the 'Erbarme dich' from the *St Matthew Passion* sounded in the auditorium, right after Dolly Parton's 'I Will Always Love You', and resulted in a lot of suppressed sobbing and sniffing. (Ellen still can't hear Bach's loveliest aria without tears in her eyes. We sit together on the sofa, and when Peter has denied his Lord for the third time and the evangelist tells how the cock crows and the cowardly disciple recalls the words of Jesus – '*Ehe der Hahn krähen wird, wirst du mich dreimal verleugnen*' – and how he goes and weeps bitterly, I take her hand and caress it and caress it and caress it until it's over and the choir comes in to comfort us both.

Bin ich gleich von dir gewichen, stell' ich mich doch wieder ein;

Hat uns doch dein Sohn verlichen durch sein Angst
    und Todespein
Ich verleugne nicht die Schuld, aber deine Gnad'
    und Huld'
Ist viel grösser als die Sünde, die ich stets in mir
    befinde.

For Bach, you don't have to be a believer. It's enough to have a heart that hasn't turned to stone.

'Niko Neerinckx has a son named Bo.'

'What do you mean?'

'Exactly what I said: Niko Neerinckx's oldest son is named Bo.'

'Niko Neerinckx isn't Bo's father, Armin.'

'He has a five-year-old son named Bo. And he keeps a picture of Monika in his family photo album.'

'What are you talking about? Where did you get that idea from? How do you know all this?'

'I paid a visit to his wife. Her name's Anke. Anke Neerinckx.'

'His wife? When? What the hell are you trying to do, Armin?'

'Find some answers. I saw Robbert, too, Robbert Hubeek, the guy Monika was with before she met me. It wasn't him, in any case. And it wasn't her doctor, either.'

'Her doctor? You suspected her doctor?' Ellen burst out laughing.

'It's not that strange.'

'But it wasn't him?'

'No.'

'So what did you ask him? How did you broach that one? Are you my son's father?'

'Exactly. But he wasn't. I also asked him whether she'd confided in him. Whether she'd ever said anything about there being someone else. But she hadn't.'

'And now you're suddenly sure it was Niko Neerinckx.'

'Yeah. Niko Neerinckx is the father of Bo. Of two Bos, to be exact.'

'My God, Armin. And you told his wife that?'

'No. Not yet.'

'Well, I wouldn't. He's not the one, Armin. Monika didn't have anything going with Niko. She wasn't interested in him at all. I'm very, very sure about that.'

'Come on, Ellen. If you don't know who it is, if you never even suspected that Monika cheated on me, then how would you know who she fell for and who she didn't? What do you really know about her, Ellen?'

'Armin, don't. It's not true.'

'So give me one good reason why I should believe you. One good reason! Do you know something I don't? No? Well, there you go! Why did Niko have to name his son Bo, even though his wife thought it was a weird name? Explain that to me, Ellen, if you know so much. Isn't it just a bit too much of a coincidence? Huh?'

'Don't, Armin.'

'Well? Answer me! You don't want to believe that Monika could ever have done anything like that. That she could have fucked the guy you were so helplessly in love with. That breaks your heart. But holy shit, Ellen, what do you think's happened to my heart? I can't hide from the truth, I can't duck away from it the way you can. I can't close my eyes! You don't know what it's like to lose your son after thirteen years. You don't know what that is, a parent's love for a child. Oh God, Ellen, don't! Don't do that! Not now! Jesus Christ!'

I left her with her tears. I went outside. Out into the rain. Rail-freight tracks used to run down the street where we live. Wagonloads of coffee and cacao and the cold carcasses from the slaughterhouse came past here. Now it's mostly moving vans, bringing in Ikea furniture for the young, ambitious couples who use this neighbourhood as a staging-post before the inevitable single-family house. We live amid the remains of a glorious past, among people full of dreams about the future. It wasn't so long ago that I still found that reassuring.

I walked until my feet hurt. Then I went back home. Ellen was still sitting on the sofa in the living room. But I went to bed without saying a word. I fell asleep right away. I dreamed I was fucking Anke Neerinckx and Ellen was watching, and that she cried and cried and cried, but I went on anyway, until Anke came, screaming. The next morning I had a splitting headache. The next morning, the place beside me in bed was empty and cold.

I go into Bo's room. He's still asleep, but when I sit down on the edge of his bed he wakes up.

'What's wrong?'

'Nothing. Ellen and I had a fight.'

He looks at me, his eyes still clouded with sleep. 'Is it bad?'

'I don't know. No. It will be all right. It always turns out all right.'

But Bo doesn't believe that. He hasn't believed that since he was three and lost his mother. He's worried. He won't look at me. He sits on the edge of his bed. He's getting big, I think. He's starting to grow hair on his calves. And suddenly panic strikes me to the heart. I can't get along without him! I must never lose him! They can't take him away from me! They. They? Who?

'Lately, you've been . . . different,' he says. 'Distracted.' He's still not looking at me. I follow his gaze. He's looking at a plated lizard sitting motionless on a rock, its head turned towards the pale morning light coming through the window. Bo has the patience of his favourite pets. Just as the lizards can wait for the moment when a fly's attention flags, Bo can wait for the moment when I lower my barriers.

'Yeah,' I say. 'The tests from the hospital got to me more than I expected.' I despise myself for lying to him – having to lie to him. 'Maybe,' I say, 'we should go somewhere together, you and me.'

He looks at me. 'The two of us? What about Ellen?'

'Ellen can take care of herself. She needs some time to think. And she'll be pleased not to see me for a while.'

'Yeah,' he says. And then, after a long silence, very guardedly, 'Yeah, that's right.'

The lizard turns its head a fraction toward the light. Then freezes again.

'Where shall we go?' he asks.

'How long are we going for?'

'A long weekend?'

'The Wadden Islands?'
'Which one?'
'Ameland?'
'Sounds good.'

'Armin is crazy,' she'd written in the sand on Ameland.

'What's it say?' Bo had asked. He'd just turned three. He asked questions all day long. I told him what his mother was asserting about his father. He was in complete agreement with her.

'Armin is crazy! Armin is crazy!' he shouted. And I threatened to feed him to the gulls, to toss him into the surf, to bury him in the wet sand. And he shrieked and laughed and ran away from me as fast as his little boots would carry him. And the sea came and washed the letters away. And suddenly his face clouded over.

'What's wrong, Bo?' Monika asked.

But he didn't answer. He grabbed her hand, and together they walked back to the dunes. And I watched them as the water rushed around my ankles and thought: I'm as happy as a man can be.

30

Bo and I are standing on the dyke at Enkhuizen. The water of the IJsselmeer is a deep, dark green. White horses and the dark shadows of clouds whip across it in fast motion. On the far shore we can see the coast of Friesland and the steeple at Stavoren.

Bo takes the binoculars and looks. The wind almost throws him off balance.

'Come on,' I say. We walk down the dyke to where the water sloshes against the black basalt. Now the dyke is between us and the worst of the wind. Bo raises the binoculars to his eyes again.

'There's a blue car driving along the dyke,' he says.

'What make?'

But he can't see it that well.

Bo has big red blotches on his cheeks, and when he hands me the binoculars his eyes are glistening. He laughs a high, giggly laugh. 'Hee hee! Hee hee hee!'

A flight of cormorants comes in low over the water, heading in our direction. Through the binoculars you can see them fighting their way into the wind.

'Bo, look,' I shout, 'cormorants!'

But Bo has already walked away. He's squatting on the basalt blocks, plucking something from between the stones with his thin, boyish fingers. That's the way it's been for years: I look at the fowls of the air, Bo looks at what's crawling beneath his feet. To see what's happening in the world right in front of us, we need other people, the way the blind need guide dogs.

I'd explained it to him at home, at the kitchen table. I took a compass and drew a circle on a piece of paper. 'Imagine this is the earth,' I said. 'Then this would be the North Pole, this is the South Pole, and here's the equator,' and I put an *N* at the top of the circle, an *S* at the bottom, and I cut the circle in half with a horizontal line.

'The experts tell us that the distance from the centre of the earth to the surface is about six thousand four hundred kilometres. That distance is called the radius. But of course it's more useful to know, for example, how far it is from the North Pole to the equator. In order to work that out you have to use a formula they say was invented by Pythagoras, an old Greek philosopher. The formula goes like this: the circumference of a circle is equal to two times the radius, multiplied by the number pi. What's the number pi? Pi is a letter in the Greek alphabet, sort of like our "p". But pi is also a number with a lot of numbers after the decimal, and it pretty much equals 3.142.'

'Oh,' Bo said.

'So, if the circumference of the circle is equal to two times the radius multiplied by pi, then it's easy to figure out the distance from the North Pole to the equator. Because then it's two times six thousand four hundred, times 3.142, divided by four.' I gave Bo the calculator and let him do the arithmetic himself.

'The distance from the North Pole to the equator,' he said solemnly, 'is ten thousand and fifty-four point four kilometres.'

'Very good,' I went on. 'At least, if Pythagoras was right. Let's check up on him.' I took a ball of string out of the cupboard and cut off a piece. 'Lay that over the circle as carefully as you can.'

The tip of his tongue protruding from between his lips, Bo did as he was told. Then we used a ruler to measure the length of the piece of twine needed to enclose the circle. And then we measured the radius of the circle.

'Now we're going to divide the circumference we just measured by two, and then by pi, or 3.142. And what do we get?'

'That's exactly how long the radius is!' Bo shouted in delight.

We drew two more circles, on blank sheets of paper, both different sizes. And again we used the string to measure the circumference and the radius. And once again, Bo entered the measurements on the calculator and did the arithmetic. And each time the result was on the button.

'That's why they called pi a divine number,' I said. 'Because it lets us make amazingly accurate predictions about the circumference of a circle, based only on what we know about the radius. And that's not all. The number pi is built into all kinds of natural phenomena. In the numerical relationship between musical notes, for example. And even in the spacing between the new leaves on a twig. But you'll find out about that in due time. Right now we're going to use it for something else.'

I poured us something to drink. A glass of cola for Bo, a whisky for myself.

'So now we know that if you walked from the North Pole to the equator, you'd cover ten thousand kilometres. And if we regard the North Pole as the highest spot on the globe, how many kilometres do you have to walk downhill, relatively speaking?'

'Six thousand four hundred!'

'Exactly! But now comes the hard part. If we put you here at the North Pole' – I drew a little stick figure beside the N – 'it seems at first as though the earth barely curves down at all. But the further you go, the steeper it gets. By the time you reach the equator, you're walking almost straight down. That's what the experts call globe-theoretical decline. Calculating that decline is really complicated, but if you know the radius, the outcome is just as predictable as the circumference of the circle – you just use a different formula. According to scientists who've done those calculations, a point here on Earth which is eight kilometres away from you, for example, is also about four metres lower. They say that's why, when a ship is sailing away from you, you can see it slowly disappear over the horizon. You'd almost think the ship was sinking into the waves, the way the ancient Greeks thought the sun disappeared over the western rim of the earth. They thought a big wagon with fiery horses was waiting there each night to take the sun to the other side of the world, so it could rise again in the east the next morning.'

'But what really happens,' Bo said, 'is that the earth spins around like a ball, and the ship doesn't disappear into the sea and the sun doesn't really go down or up.'

'Exactly!'

Bo took a sip of cola and said, 'Is that all you were going to teach me? I already knew the earth is a ball. And that ships don't sink on the horizon, but drop away 'cause the sea is curved, just like the land.'

'All right, but I haven't finished yet,' I said. 'You see, there's a real problem here. After all, globe-theoretical decline increases with distance, as we saw with that circle we drew. At eight kilometres, the decline is only four metres, but at sixteen kilometres it's not eight any more, it's twenty. And at twenty kilometres it's thirty-five. In other words, based on calculations that assume a round earth, it should be impossible to see a dyke, a house or even a church steeple at any great distance. Tomorrow we're going to try it for ourselves. How about going to get your atlas?'

Bo slid off his chair and ran to his room. He didn't even have to turn on the light to find the atlas.

'Turn to the map of Holland. You see Enkhuizen? And Stavoren?'

Bo pointed to the two towns on the map.

'What's the distance between them?' Using his ruler and the scale at the bottom of the map, Bo had no trouble calculating the distance.

'A little over twenty kilometres.'

'Good. That means the globe-theoretical decline must be a little over thirty-five metres. Which means that from

Enkhuizen, even on top of the dyke, you shouldn't be able to see Stavoren. Tomorrow we'll go to Enkhuizen, to see if the theory really explains reality.'

'Dad, does this mean the world is actually flat?' Bo asks in the car on the way home.

'I don't think so, Bo. Everyone agrees that the earth is round. At least, almost everyone. You can see it in pictures taken from outer space. But the important thing to remember is that people think they know a lot of things, but mostly all they do is believe them. At school they teach you that the world is round, so everyone says they know it's true. I once asked my geography teacher why you can see Stavoren from the dyke at Enkhuizen. "But Armin," he said, "that's quite simple." He started by drawing something on the board. That was just after class started. By the end of the period, the board was covered with arithmetic. The teacher's face was red as a beet, sweat was running down his face, but he still hadn't been able to answer my question. Two days later I ran into him in the hall. "Ah, Armin Minderhout," he said. "About the dyke at Stavoren. I've been thinking about it, and the answer, of course, is that you can see it from Enkhuizen because of reflections in the atmosphere. It's a fata Morgana, in fact. A bit silly of me not to think of it before, but at least now you can relax. Take it from me, the earth really *is* round, not flat, not the way you seemed to think there for a moment." And Bo, that's exactly what people do: they assume things are a certain way because some authority has told them so, and because other people agree that it's true. Whether it really is, whether things really are the way we believe, most people don't have the foggiest. Don't ever forget that.'

31

My father is dead.

The phone rang.

'Am I speaking to Mr Minderhout? Mr Minderhout, your father is dead.'

It's my father's neighbour, a retired civil servant who had worked for the national tax office and used to help my father fill in his tax return each year in exchange for a bottle of good wine.

'He's sitting across from me in his chair at the window, your father,' he says. 'I was taking Boris for a walk. I saw him sitting here and I waved, but he didn't wave back. I thought: he's probably daydreaming about Marijke again. He misses your mother every day, is what he says. But when I went past again he was still sitting here like this. And he still didn't see me. So I thought: there's something wrong. I went around to the back of the house. The door was unlocked. I told Boris, "Boris, stay!" Poor mutt didn't understand. But I thought: I don't want that animal around. I had a feeling about it. The lamp in the living room was still on. So I turned it off. He must have been sitting here all night. His glass of wine's still on the table. Half full. Or half empty. Depends on how you look at it.

A Burgundy. Your father still has a couple of very nice Burgundies.'

He won't stop talking.

'Yesterday's post is on the table. Two bank statements and a prospectus from a building-materials company. He was reading a book. Something religious. I didn't know your father was religious. But, well, when we get older and we start . . . I mean, maybe he felt it coming, who knows? You read about things like that sometimes. Bach knew what day he was going to . . . They say he worked that date into a lot of his compositions. I don't know anything about music, of course, I just read that somewhere. Years ago. But I never forgot it. Sometimes that happens, with that kind of thing. You keep thinking about it for ages. You read something like that and you think: is that really possible?'

I can hear a dog whining in the background.

'All right, I'm coming! That's Boris. He doesn't understand what's going on, poor puppy. I left him outside. I thought: don't need that dog around. Mr Minderhout?'

'Yes.'

'I was thinking: I couldn't hear you any more. I mean, maybe it would be good if you . . . I mean.'

'I'm coming,' I say. 'Go to Boris. I'm coming. I'll ring your bell when I get there.'

'Oh, that's great. Yeah, that's great.' He sounds relieved. The panic leaves his voice. 'You don't have to rush. I mean . . .'

'That's fine, Mr Bruggeman. Thank you very much. I'm coming.'

* * *

Ellen is at work.

Bo is at school.

My father is dead.

I ring Ellen and tell her the bad news.

'I'll be right there,' she says.

'No, I'll pick you up. We can drive over there together.'

She's nice to me when she gets in the car. In a way
only she can be nice. With a little gesture, a touch, a
phrase.

'You can get used to almost anything. But not to
things you don't see coming.'

We drive to Abcoude. There's a parking space in front
of the door. My father sits there watching as I back the
car into place. I misjudge the distance to the kerb. The
right rear tyre scrapes against cement. There are yellow
daffodils in flower under the front window. It takes a
long time for me to work up the courage to get out
of the car. My father doesn't get up. He doesn't open
the door.

My father is dead. I believe it's slowly starting to
sink in.

Boris, a black fluffy mongrel, barks and jumps excitedly
against the frosted glass of Mr Bruggeman's front door.
It takes a minute for the old man himself to appear. He
looks pale, and his hands are shaking. At his age, he must
be thinking that he's next. (I think: wasn't it actually his
turn? Isn't it immediately obvious that he should have
gone before my father? But fate decided differently. In
my life, fate often decides differently.)

'Mr Minderhout. Ma'am,' he says. 'I'm glad you're here. Please come in. Boris, get down! Sit! Good dog! Your father . . .'

'We saw him.'

'Yes, of course. Boris, c'mere!' The dog, which was barking loudly and wagging its tail on the way to the door again, comes back into the room. The old man shuffles into the kitchen, opens a jar and takes out a few chunks of dried dog food.

'Sit.' The dog sits.

'Stay.' The man picks up a white enamelled bowl with DOGGY printed on it in red letters. The dog peeps and sticks its tongue out. But it doesn't move. The man puts the bowl on the ground, and the dog still waits.

'Get it!' And the animal pounces greedily on the dog food.

We walk out of the living room, into the hallway, and Mr Bruggeman closes the door behind him. At the end of the hall is a door to the garden. He walks out in front of us.

'Be sure to pull the door shut behind you,' he says. 'These days Boris can open the hall door.'

As we walk into the garden we indeed hear a latch being pushed down with a bang, then excited barking from the hall. Boris's black head appears at the window of the back door. All three of us have to laugh about that. Then we're standing in my father's garden. There's a crate of violets still waiting to be planted. Mr Bruggeman opens the back door and goes inside. At the door to the living room, he stops.

'Please, you first,' he says. We sidle past him, first

Ellen, then me. We walk into the room and look at the dead man in the chair by the window. It is undeniably my father. But it's undeniably no longer him, either. There's a strange smell in the room, or maybe I'm imagining it, but Ellen also seems to hesitate before approaching the dead body. She waits until I'm next to her. She takes my hand. I know she never thought much of my father. She said his self-assured air annoyed her. 'He acts as though he accepts me, but he only tolerates me at best.'

I never worried too much about what she thought of him. The contact between my father and me was never that close. Only in the last few years, after my mother died, did we start seeing each other a bit more. Maybe because we were in the same boat again. Because we were each other's equals again: widowers both.

'From the looks of it, he didn't suffer.' Mr Bruggeman is the first to break the silence.

'No,' Ellen says. 'He just fell asleep.' She steps closer. 'Shall we close his eyes?'

'Try it,' I say.

'Don't you want to do it?'

'No, rather not.'

She closes his eyes. I see her shiver.

'He's cold and stiff.'

'Shall we lay him on his bed?' Mr Bruggeman asks. You can tell from his voice that he hopes we'll say no.

'No,' I say. 'Let him sit like this. I'll ring the undertakers, and they'll take care of everything.'

'I already threw away what was left in his wineglass,' Mr Bruggeman says. 'And I washed the glass. And I put that book back on the shelf.'

'Thank you,' Ellen says. She's still holding my hand. 'Do you want me to ring?'

'No, I'll do it.'

I find the phone book and look up the number of the undertakers who arranged my mother's funeral. They promise to send someone over right away. Within an hour, we're all sitting at the kitchen table, discussing the things that have to be discussed at a moment like this, just as we did two years ago. It's even the same man. Only my father isn't in on this conversation. He's sitting in his chair, his eyes closed. Everything he wanted to say about his funeral he put down carefully on paper. The man from the undertakers reads it to us in a quiet, sympathetic voice. When he gets to the part about the music and mentions 'Ave Maria', which they also played at my mother's funeral, I feel a sudden chill. Under the table, Ellen lays a hand on my leg.

'Your father wants to be cremated,' the man says.

I never knew that.

There aren't many people at the ceremony.

From behind the lectern, I let my gaze run over their faces. An uncle and an aunt, old and grey and with death in their eyes, a number of unfamiliar faces (probably former employees of my father's contracting company), two nieces, one pretty and thin but sloppy, the other fat and ugly but dressed to a tee. Their husbands, whom I last saw at my mother's funeral, apparently didn't think it was worth taking time off from work this time, and who am I to blame them? I hate funerals, I'll seize any excuse not to attend them. For this one, though, there was no excuse at hand.

I look at Ellen and Bo, sitting beside each other in the front row. Ellen nods encouragingly. It's about time I said something.

'I've had thirty-six years to prepare myself for this day,' I say. 'It wasn't long enough. What can you say at your own father's cremation? That you'll miss him? That he was important to you? That you loved him, even at those moments when you hated him? That you regularly catch yourself saying things to your son that he used to say to you? It's all true, but what good is it?'

Bo looks at the tips of his shoes. Ellen looks at me. The two nieces look at the coffin. Mr Bruggeman looks at his hands lying folded in his lap. Again the thought flashes through my mind: he's the one who should have died, not my father. That's what I'd really like to say, but I don't.

I say, 'I'm not going to try to sum up my father in a few words. I would be doing him an injustice, and doing all of you an injustice, and ultimately doing myself an injustice as well. A person's life can't be captured in words; good thing, too. So what else is there to say? A few days ago someone said to me, "You can get used to anything, but not to what you don't see coming." And that's how it is. You can get used to anything, but not to death.'

When 'Ave Maria' is played, I'm the only one who cries. (Bo is sitting next to me. I hear him gulp, but he doesn't cry.) Ellen puts her hand on my leg again. When I look at her, she puckers her lips for just a moment, as if she wants to soften my pain with a kiss, the way mothers do with little children.

My father is dead, I think. He's lying there in that box and in a little while they'll burn him. So who do I have left? Ellen and Bo. Will that be enough? The year I drank myself to the edge of the abyss, yes, they were enough for me then – at least, enough to make me stop and turn back right before the edge.

My drinking started when, after two months of hard work and denial, I finally admitted to myself that Monika was dead. At first I drank mostly in cafés, often with Dees, often with Bo, sometimes completely alone. Then I started drinking at home, too. Whisky, mostly, and red wine. Within a few months I was living a life that would have finished me if Ellen hadn't been there. She's the one who saved me. She and Bo. There were nights when I would sit in a bar with Bo until four in the morning, and then wander through the city for hours, with him asleep on my back. I got into arguments with other drunkards and vagrants, and it was only because of the toddler on my back that it never really turned ugly.

One early summer morning, Bo and I were sitting on a bench in the Sarphatipark. I'd been roaming all night again, and Bo had just woken up. We looked at the ducks in the pond, and Bo asked why ducks quack and coots peep.

I had no idea.

Then he asked me why coots moved their heads back and forth like that when they swam, and ducks didn't. Again, I had no idea. We didn't say anything for a while.

Two drakes were chasing a female around the pond. 'Why are they doing that?' Bo asked. Fortunately, this time I knew the answer. 'Because the males,' I said, 'are bored to death. That's because they get so much to eat from people who come here to feed the ducks. Normally, ducks spend most of the day looking for food. But city ducks have a cushy life: they don't have to look for food, because it's thrown to them by nice people like you and me. So they have a lot of time to do other things. The only problem is, ducks don't have a very good imagination. They don't know what to do with all that free time. The only thing they can come up with is to chase the females. So that's what they do. Sometimes the drakes chase a female around so much, she finally drowns.'

Bo thought that was pretty terrible. 'We shouldn't feed them any more,' he said.

'Maybe you're right, maybe we shouldn't.'

'What about gulls?' he asked then. 'Do gulls do that too?'

'No, they don't do that.'

'Good,' Bo said.

Right then I saw Ellen coming into the park. I hadn't seen her since the day of Monika's funeral, eight months earlier. She'd rung me twice, but I'd been abrupt and said I'd ring her when I was feeling better. But the months went by and I never rang. In fact, I wasn't feeling better.

She was wearing jogging pants, but she wasn't jogging.

'Let's go,' I said to Bo.

I had no idea whether she'd seen us, but I knew for certain that she hadn't seen that we'd seen her. She could still consider it a coincidence that I was hurrying away from her. Bo and I left the park and crossed the Ceintuurbaan to our house. At the front door I glanced over my shoulder. Ellen was nowhere in sight. But we were barely inside when the bell rang.

I hesitated for a long time about opening the door, but I suspected that she'd actually seen me, which would have made it very impolite not to answer. And besides, what possible reason could I have to avoid her? I didn't know myself. Or I didn't want to know.

I opened the door. She was standing at the bottom of the steps. 'Hi, it's me. Can I come up?'

'Better not. It's such a mess here.' That was true. It was an awful mess.

'I want to talk to you. Want to hear how you're doing. And Bo.'

'Yes. Good. Or, reasonable. Thanks.'

She remained standing there indecisively. A tram bell clanged.

'I was in the neighbourhood.'

'You know what?' I said. 'You know that taxi drivers' café, just down the Ceintuurbaan? There are always a couple of cabs in front of it at this time of day. You can't miss it. Let's meet there. In fifteen minutes. Make it twenty.'

'Okay,' she said.

But fifteen minutes later, after I'd shaved and combed my hair and put on clean clothes, and while I was trying to put some clean clothes on Bo as well, he threw himself on the sofa, shrieking. He kicked and punched me and shouted, 'I don't want to, I don't want to!' And no matter how I tried to calm him, there was nothing I could do. The fatigue was taking its toll. I was angry and desperate and sad and ashamed of my impotence, and so I went into the kitchen and poured myself a whisky and sat down in a chair by the window and drank and waited and drank.

When the phone rang, I didn't answer. And twenty minutes later, when the doorbell rang for the second time that morning, I didn't open the door. Bo had fallen asleep on the sofa by then, and a little later I fell asleep, too. When I woke up late that afternoon, Bo was sitting there, holding my glass of whisky to his lips. Very carefully, he took a sip. And started coughing terribly right away.

I picked him up and held him tight and I comforted him and promised him I would straighten out my life and get rid of all the nasty drink in the house, and that we wouldn't spend any more nights in bars and that we'd start feeding the ducks in the park again, as we used to, but he didn't want that, and only then, very slowly, did the memories of that morning come back, and I picked up the phone and rang Ellen. But Ellen wasn't there.

The coffin sinks slowly into a space below the room. Then the floor closes. And that's that. I cry without stopping, without a sound, without tears. I shake hands.

'My condolences.'

'Thank you.'

'My condolences.'

'Thank you, too.'

'My condolences.'

'My condolences.'

'My condolences.'

'My condolences.'

Of all the shitty words in the language, there's no shittier word than 'condolences'.

32

On deck, out of the wind and in the sun, it's warm enough for us to take off our jackets. We left the car at the harbour. Our backpacks are between us on the hardwood bench. A dark-brown plume of smoke drifts over our heads towards the mainland. Gulls glide along with us, their wings motionless. A child gets a piece of bread from its mother and holds it out for the birds at arm's length. A huge herring gull swerves closer. Within a few inches of the child's hand, it hangs in the air. Effortlessly. Its cold eye assesses the situation. Then it strikes, fast as lightning. Immediately, a couple of other gulls start shrieking loudly and the chase begins.

The child starts crying.

Bo laughs and glances over at me. Our eyes meet. Nothing else is necessary.

Eider ducks are bobbing in the harbour at Nes, the young males half in beautiful white array, half in the sombre brown of the female of their species, as though they dressed in a hurry this morning. We take the bus to Hollum, where we've rented a house, or rather part of a house, the old entrance hall of a renovated farm. It has two little bedrooms, one barely big enough for a double bed, the other a single with a window looking out on a stone wall. Bo automatically puts his things in the little room.

'Don't you want to sleep in a nice big bed for once?' I ask.

He hesitates for a moment.

'Yeah,' he says then. He picks up his backpack and tosses it in a graceful arc onto the double bed in the room across the little corridor. The pack bounces and Bo drops onto his back beside it.

'Not bad,' he says.

I put my bag in the empty cabinet that's been squeezed in between wall and bed in the little room, and test my own, narrow mattress.

'Nice and hard,' I shout.

He comes and stands in the doorway, a broad grin on his face.

'What?' I ask.

'I could get used to this.'

I throw a pillow at his head. He ducks.

'Coffee?' he shouts from the kitchen.

Besides Amsterdam, the islands are the only place in Holland where I can truly be happy. The sea, the wind, the space, and above all the changelessness. From the bus I didn't see one building that hadn't been there ten years ago, the last time Monika and I were here. They've built a new cycle path, or maybe just repaved the old one, but that's the only sign of progress. I hate 'progress' – it's a worn-out excuse for ugliness. 'You're even more conservative than your old dad,' Ellen always says, and she's right. My father could wax lyrical about the craftsmanship of a Louis XVI chair, but when he furnished his own kitchen he opted for plastic folding chairs from Ikea. 'Easy to store, and easy to keep clean.' I don't have anything against Ikea, but why do they have to make bright-blue and hard-yellow stores that clash so loudly with the green Dutch landscape? After all, even without those colours we'd know it's a Swedish company, wouldn't we? And besides, aren't all the chairs and sofas, carpets and duvets piled up inside in such staggering quantities mostly made by underpaid workers in tropical low-wage countries? But my father said you couldn't shoulder the suffering of the whole world, that you had to keep life simple. Fighting against progress, he said, was as senseless as complaining about the weather. He was right. But still. Dying is also a form of progress, and fighting against death is also as futile as complaining about the weather, but does that mean we should welcome death with open arms? Next week I'll have to clear out his house. The plastic chairs from Ikea, the bed where he slept with my mother, the chair he died in. That he won't be there to tell me how to lift things and how I should take the bookcase apart and which clothes should be got rid of and which absolutely not – is that progress?

We drink the coffee Bo made – in the ugly white-and-grey speckled coffee machine on the equally ugly plastic counter – from Old Dutch cups with Old Dutch pictures of church steeples and cantilever bridges, and we eat the shortbread biscuits I'd brought along for the crossing but which we never got to, in the spring sunshine on the calm waters of the Wadden Shallows, busy as we were with the aerial acrobatics of the gulls.

'What are we going to do first?' I ask Bo when we've finished our coffee. 'Go to the beach, or out on to the mudflats?'

'Is it low tide?' he asks in turn.

Good question. That's another reason why I love the islands: on the islands, nature is still important. Whether the tide is out or in. Whether the wind is pounding the water against the dyke, or against the dunes. Whether the moon is bright enough to go looking for owls. Whether the lapwing is brooding. Whether the brent-geese have come back, or just left for their nesting grounds in western Siberia.

We decide to go to the shallows. We'll see what the tide's doing. (When we arrived on the ferry it was low tide, but was the tide *already* low, or was it *still* low? – stupid city slickers don't notice details like that.) I take my binoculars along, and Bo has the old biscuit tin in which he puts the curios he somehow finds in the tall grass, beneath dense shrubbery, in the nooks and crannies between brick or basalt blocks on every walk we take.

As we climb up onto the dyke, amid the sheep and the screeching lapwings (they're brooding), I think about how easy it is here to forget about all the cares you had in the city. Here, where nothing changes but the weather and the tides, it's easy to go back in time. (Is that the only reason why I abhor progress, because I want to go back in time? I don't dare answer that.)

We're in luck: the mudflats are empty and dry.

We stand beside each other on the dyke and look at the world at our feet. Above a shivering line of white light, we see the Frisian coast suspended on the horizon.

'How far away is that, as the crow flies?' Bo asks.

'About ten kilometres.'

'An eight-metre decline.'

'Give or take a bit.'

'A fata Morgana.'

'Precisely.' And we laugh and walk down the dyke and step onto the thick, greasy mud. A pair of oystercatchers fly up, protesting loudly.

We walk for a while in the direction of the Frisian mainland, saying nothing. I search for words to describe the smell of the shallows, but can't find them. Then Bo says, 'What I don't understand is why, when you're in a polder, you never see half a church steeple. Or half a utility tower.'

'What?'

'I mean, when a yacht goes away from the coast, you see it slowly disappearing over the horizon, right? Until all you can see is the top of the mast – at least, that's what they say. But why does that only happen at sea? It has to apply to dry land too, doesn't it? In Flevoland you can easily look all the way to the horizon, but I've never seen half a utility tower sticking up. Why not?'

I look at him, astonished. I had never thought of that.

'If you ask me, that's an excellent question for your geography teacher.'

We walk on across the brown, muddy flats until we

arrive at a channel where invisible fish are cutting V-patterns in the shallow water.

'What do you think?'

'Mullet?'

'That's what I think, too.'

We've caught them before, Bo and I, those fast, round fish. With a borrowed fly rod, using a green fly that was supposed to look like a piece of floating algae. Their fighting was spectacular, they jumped out of the water, sprinted impressively. And they tasted good, too.

We stand there for a while, staring longingly at the movement just below the surface, until suddenly the silence around us is broken by shouts. From the west, five figures are approaching, silhouetted against the pale spring sky. The wind blows in snatches of excited conversation. A high girlish laugh. A boy's voice shouting 'Coward' or 'Bastard'. As though we've been caught doing something, Bo and I start walking at the same moment. The channel bends off in the direction of the five young people. Three girls. Two boys.

'Hello,' one of the boys says when we get near. 'Have you seen any seals around these parts?'

'No,' I reply.

'But you do have them around here, don't you?' one of the girls asks.

'Sometimes,' Bo says.

'See?' the girl says. 'You just don't know anything about nature!' And she smiles at Bo and says, 'Those black and white birds with the orange bills, those are oystercatchers, right?'

'That's right,' Bo says.

'See? Thank you very much.'

And then they walk on, the boys a little quieter now, the girls a little louder.

Bo remains standing and digs the tip of his boot into the mud. I walk on a few paces, then turn around and wait for him. I see the girl who asked him about the oystercatchers glance back over her shoulder. She's wearing a black baseball cap, and her eyes glisten in the half-shadow of the visor.

'She was flirting with you,' I say.

But Bo doesn't say a word. He pulls something shiny out of the mud and puts it in his tin.

33

Ellen rolls onto her side and pulls the duvet up over her bare breasts. The smell of sex hangs over us like a reassurance. Her feet are stroking mine. For the first time in weeks, the glass wall that's separated us since we heard the test results has vanished. For the first time, when I came I didn't think: how senseless!

I don't know whether it's ever been the object of study (can't imagine it hasn't), but I believe that people who have just been to a funeral have a much greater need for sex than usual. Death as aphrodisiac. Sex as a way to thumb your nose at the Grim Reaper: look at us celebrating life, you can't keep us down!

'What are you thinking about?' Ellen asks.

'About that other time, after another funeral.'

'Do you still regret that?'

'No . . . no, not regret. But.'

'But what?'

'But this time it wasn't just the two of us, either.'

'There were three of us.'

'Yeah.'

'Did you think about her, too?'

'Yeah.'

We're both silent. Her hand strokes my side, my chest. I close my eyes and think about Monika. Ten years – and still not dead and buried. I feel a tear running down my cheek, hanging on my chin for a moment, hesitating, then dripping onto my chest. Ellen kisses my forehead, my eyes, my nose, my cheeks, my mouth. I pull her up close.

'Go ahead and cry,' she says. 'Just cry.'

And I push my face into her hair. I kiss her neck. I kiss my own tears off her breast. I lay my head on her belly, which is moist and sticky.

'Dear Armin, poor, dear Armin.'

'Kiss me, just kiss me.'

And she kisses me and strokes me. She embraces me. She squeezes me. And then her heart breaks. Then the dykes break behind which she's been hiding her sorrow for weeks. I feel her body bucking beneath the violent stream of emotions. I hold her tight. I stroke her hair, her back, I press her against me with all the strength I have in my body.

'Go ahead and cry,' I say. 'Just cry.'

And she cries and cries and cries, and this time I can comfort her. At least I've achieved that much in the space of ten years: that I don't kick her away from me, like a cornered animal.

She was sitting on the edge of the bed. Naked and sweaty and stunned.

'Out of here!' I screamed. 'Go! Go! Go! Goddamn it, what are you doing here!?' I picked her clothes off the floor and threw them in her face. 'Get dressed!'

I hopped into my jeans, pulled a sweater over my head. She stayed on the edge of the bed, as though she was drugged.

'Get dressed!' I screamed again. I grabbed her by the shoulders and pulled her to her feet. And she awoke from her state of shock and pushed me aside with gentle force and got dressed. Calmly and efficiently.

'I'm sorry,' she said at the door; then she turned and left. I tore the sheets off the bed and stuffed them into the washing machine. In the hall I found an earring that must have fallen in among the sheets and I picked it up and went into the bedroom and opened the window and threw the earring away. Then I undressed and had a shower and scrubbed myself with soap and water so hot I could barely stand it. Very gradually, I grew calmer, and after I'd dried off I put on Monika's bathrobe and sat on the sofa and rang my mother and asked, 'How's Bo doing?'

'He's asleep. How are you doing?'

'Good. Bad.'

'Are you sure you don't want to sleep over here?'

'Yes, I'm sure.'

But I didn't dare to go back into the bedroom again that night. I stayed on the sofa and buried my face in the folds of the bathrobe that still smelled of Monika, who we had buried that morning.

I'd bought ten bunches of white roses at the market on the Albert Cuypstraat. And Bo and I had cut the blossoms from the stems and put them in the little plastic bucket Bo played with wherever there was sand.

'These flowers are for Mama.'

'When do I give them to her?'

'Tomorrow. Tomorrow morning.'

And that morning, at the side of the freshly dug

grave into which the undertaker's men had just low-
ered the coffin, I said to Bo, 'Shall we give her the
flowers now?'

'Okay.'

Bo had dipped his little hand into the bucket, and
when the first rosebuds landed with a soft thud on the
lid of the coffin I heard Monika's mother burst into tears
behind us, but we didn't pay any attention and we went
on tossing the flowers in until the bucket was empty and
Bo took a step forward and said, 'Bye, Mama.' And I
took him by the hand and together we walked back
to the auditorium, to the coffee and the cake and the
condolences. Monika's parents accepted condolences,
but condoled with no one themselves. All they did was
pick up Bo for a moment. They almost squeezed him
flat. Then they left without saying goodbye.

When it was all over, my mother said, 'Come with
us.' And I said, 'If I don't go home now, I never will.
But maybe Bo can sleep at your place tonight, so I don't
have to worry about him?'

And so Bo went with my parents. He nodded very
understandingly when I said that Grandma and Grandpa
Minderhout could take care of him today better than I
could. I had someone call me a taxi. And Ellen, who had
come with a colleague from Small World, said, 'I'll give
you a ring this evening.' But instead of phoning, a couple
of hours later she was standing on my doorstep.

'I was going crazy at home. But if you'd rather be
alone, just say so.'

'I'm glad you're here,' I answered, and I was, because
without Bo and without Monika the house suddenly

seemed an enemy, a place where memories were being shot at me from every corner, like poisoned arrows.

We cooked together, ate together, opened a bottle of wine together, stared at the TV together without seeing a thing, thought about Monika together without saying a word.

'Can I sleep here tonight?' Ellen asked.

'Sure, that's okay.'

And we crawled into bed and Ellen clamped onto me and I rolled her onto her back and lay on top of her and she spread her legs and pressed her pelvis against mine and I closed my eyes and thought Monika, Monika, Monika, and she dug her nails into my back and bit me on the shoulder and I shuddered from the pain and the pleasure and the rage and the sorrow and my hands slid under her buttocks and I forced my way into her, and she shivered and groaned and clutched at me as a drowning person clutches a rescuer and when she came all the strength poured out of her body and she began crying and I straightened up and looked at the teary face, and a desperate, irrational rage overcame me and I pulled out of her and jumped out of bed and she sat up, startled, naked and shivering and still sobbing, and I shouted and shouted and shouted.

Post-mortem sex is a complicated form of sadomaso-chism.

'You mustn't run away any more when we fight,' Ellen says when the crying is over.

'No,' I say. 'I'm sorry.'

'I was so afraid you were going to throw me out of the house.'

'Me, throw you out? Why would I do that?'

'To beat me to it. Because you're afraid I'm going to leave you, because you can't give me a child.'

I drop back onto my pillow.

'Am I right?'

I sigh and nod. 'Maybe you should find someone to make you pregnant.'

'Don't be stupid.'

'I'm very good at it, you know. Raising other people's children, I mean.'

She laughs, but only halfheartedly. 'Poor Armin.'

I look at her. She looks tired. Sad, too. She's thirty-four. She'd make a good mother. She *is* a good mother. For Bo. But Bo isn't her child. I say, 'You're not too bad at it, either.'

'At what?'

'Raising other people's children.'

'Strange that never occurred to me before.'

'What?'

'That now we're equals in that way. That we're raising someone else's child together.'

'Her child.'

'Yeah, her child.'

34

Bo cooked the supper. Potatoes with broccoli and fish sticks. I made the salad, and poured the white wine. Now we're sitting at the table by the window. Outside, night is slowly falling. A farmer comes past on his bicycle and waves. Island life.

We drink a toast. 'To island life,' I say.

'Do you remember,' Bo says, 'that time the three of us went fishing? Grandpa, you and me?'

I remember.

'He wasn't much good at it.'

'He was lousy at it.'

'Yeah. But he caught the biggest bream of the day.'

'Beginner's luck.'

'Yeah, beginner's luck.'

It must have been about eight years ago. Around the time Ellen moved in with us. Bo and I had become desperately addicted to fishing (which, after all the alcohol, was a real improvement for me). Hardly a weekend went by without the two of us going out. During the fishing I taught Bo the difference between the song of the reed warbler and that of the great reed warbler, the difference between the hen harrier and Montague's harrier. I told him about the cuckoo that lays its eggs in another bird's nest. And about the inhabitants of Borneo, who believe you can predict the future by the flight of birds. I told him about the great mysteries of the earliest civilizations.

'Six thousand years ago,' I said, 'members of a Neolithic tribe in south-west England built a huge calculator that's known today as the monument at Stonehenge. According to official archaeological accounts, it's a temple where sacrifices were made to the nature gods of the day. But Stonehenge is much more than that. It's also a sundial and a moon gate. It's a mathematical model of the universe as we perceive it from Earth. Precise measurements have shown that the builders of Stonehenge were familiar with the wondrous properties of right-angled triangles, and that they knew of the divine number pi. They must have been able to predict lunar eclipses and solstices, as well as solar eclipses and the movements of the tides. There's only one little problem: according to the history of Western civilization, there was no way those Stone Age barbarians could have known all that. Which is why all the amazing discoveries about Stonehenge haven't made it into the official textbooks.'

'Are we going to go there some time, to Stonehenge?' Bo asked.

I said we would, and not long ago I reminded myself to finally keep that promise.

That was the kind of thing I told Bo as we stared at our floats. That, and a lot more. I told him about the madness of the arms race, and about the blasphemy of Christian politicians who used clever loopholes to keep their millions out of the hands of the tax department, and about the arrogance of the men who ran the multinational oil companies and did business with the apartheid regime in South Africa just as offhandedly as they justified polluting the environment. And I told him about his mother. About the whiteness of her skin and the red of her hair. About how angry she was when she read the articles I edited for the publishing house, in which laboratory animals were tortured and killed for scientific purposes. And Bo asked, 'So why do they do that, torture animals?'

And I said, 'To test medicines, for example. Medicines that could save people's lives.'

And Bo said, 'But not her life.'

'No, not her life.'

One day my father said, 'I'd like to go along some time, when the two of you go fishing. I want to see what's such fun about it.'

My father had never understood what I saw in fishing. (In fact, my father had never understood much about me. Until the day I came home with Monika.)

'How do you keep from getting bored to death, sitting there by the water?' my father had always asked.

'Don't you get cold?'

'Aren't you embarrassed, walking down the street with one of those rods?'

'Don't you realize that you'll never find some sweet young thing with a crusty old hobby like that?'

'And then that bird-watching business. God only knows how you came up with that aberration; you didn't get it from me, anyway.'

That I'd somehow succeeded in latching on to Monika remained a true mystery to my father, but it undeniably boosted my status in his eyes. And when I got her pregnant – but, well, I've already talked about that. Just as I've talked about how everything reverted when Monika died. As though Monika had been a pair of spectacles my father needed in order to see his own son as an adult. That I started fishing again a few years after she died only made things worse. I'd become that strange son of his again who refused to succeed in life. I'd become my mother's child again.

It was just like my father to catch the biggest fish of the day. In the same way it was just like my father to impress Bo the whole day with hilarious stories about the construction business and backroom municipal politics, and about the fraudulent practices of aldermen and bribes and drinking parties.

'You remember his story about that tax inspector?' Bo says.

I remembered.

'Boy, did he make me laugh.'

It was a story my father told many times after that, at birthday parties and during Christmas dinners. It was a story that ended with a drunken tax auditor leaving his dossier in a seedy nightclub, and then calling my father meekly the next day and asking whether he'd seen it. But my father had feigned ignorance, and nothing ever came of *The People* v. *Minderhout Construction*.

'Why didn't you two get along?' Bo asks suddenly.

'We got along.'

'No you didn't. Not like we get along.'

'No, not like that, no. He was . . .' I try to find the right words. 'When I was a kid he always made me feel

that I was a lot less than he was. That I'd never be able
to do all the things he did. And he was right. He was
one of those people who can do anything.'

'He couldn't fish.'

'You're right, but he still caught the biggest fish.
Which was just like him.'

'He wasn't very brave.'

'What do you mean?'

'He was always shooting off his mouth, but in fact he
was really scared. Scared of things changing.'

I look at him, the way he's sitting there across from
me. Just turned fourteen. Sipping his wine carefully.

'What makes you think that?'

He shrugs. 'Everything. After Grandma died, there
wasn't much left of him.'

Well well. The grandson has spoken. (The grandson?)
I burst out laughing.

'What is it?' he asks.

'Nothing.'

'So why are you laughing?'

'Because you're right. Because you say things I wouldn't
dare to say in that way.'

'Because he's your father,' Bo says understandingly.

'*Was* my father.'

'Yeah, was, of course.'

35

I kept Ellen at a distance for a long time. (I also kept drinking for a long time). A few days after she'd knocked on our door in vain, and after the evening I'd tried to ring her in vain, she finally picked up the phone. I apologized for my antisocial behaviour, she said 'It's okay,' and she invited us over for dinner. We went and we talked and we laughed and we drank in moderation. And Bo and I went home on time, and when we said goodbye we kissed each other on the cheek.

Weeks went by in which we didn't see or speak to each other, but then suddenly she would be at the door and I would let her in and we would talk again and laugh again and drink in moderation, and we always said goodbye in the proper way: as friends. Sometimes she would take Bo to the park, or the zoo. Sometimes Bo slept over at her place. (I'd met someone at the disco. I wasn't in love with her, but she was in love with me, and I used that to sleep with her when I felt like it – which in the long run wasn't often enough to keep her satisfied, and she left me. Which made me much sadder than I cared to admit.)

Ellen also had a brief relationship, with another man. I told her I was happy for her, and that she deserved all the love in the world. Nevertheless, when he broke up with her and she didn't seem to be suffering too much,

I was relieved. And the next time that Bo and I went to visit her I took along a bottle of champagne, to celebrate freedom regained.

Time went by and my life resumed its normal course. I started drinking less, and Bo spent more time at school and made friends with whom he went to play or sleep the night. I was back to editing texts about the effect of oxalate on the gluconeogenesis of isolated chicken hepatocytes, and other exalted themes. Along with Dees I waited with bated breath for the results of research into the molecular similarities between such diverse species as the fruit fly, the carp, the pig and the human being.

'What it's all about,' Dees explained to me, 'is the structure of the protein cytochrome C. It's a protein found in almost all living organisms, so it was expected that a correlation would be found between the extent to which that protein differs from one species to the next and the geological points at which those species arose. Species relatively close on the evolutionary ladder should resemble each other more closely in terms of protein structure than species more widely removed. After all, the differences are caused by random mutations. So the more time between the appearance of two species, the greater the differences should be. At least, that's what people thought. But it doesn't work that way. The cytochrome C of the carp, for example, is sixty-four per cent identical to that of *Rhodospirillum rubrum* bacteria. The same goes for the pig. And the cytochrome C of human beings and fruit flies is actually sixty-five per cent identical to that of the bacteria. Which means,' and here Dees's voice took on a triumphant air, 'that from the point of view of the *Rhodospirillum rubrum* bacteria, human beings are as close or as distant kin as the fruit fly. A rather nasty blow for evolutionary theory.'

As a counterweight to work and family life, and to the stimulating but rather demanding conversations with Dees, I plunged headlong into two long, hot, summer months of nightlife. I had several one-night stands, and for a while there even thought I'd fallen in love. (With a girl with red hair, who was at the police academy and voted European Liberal. 'It'll never last,' Ellen chortled, and it didn't.) And just when I thought: there will never be anyone else for me but Monika, and so be it, just then, of course, it happened anyway.

'You started it,' Ellen would say later.

'No one started it,' I said. 'As usual.'

Six months later she moved in with us.

'Is it okay if Ellen comes to live with us?' I asked Bo.

He thought it was okay.

My mother cried with joy when she heard about it. And my father said he was happy for me, too, but in everything he did I noticed that Ellen didn't impress him the way Monika had. And Ellen noticed it, too. In any case, she always maintained a certain reserve towards my father.

'I just don't get along too well with that kind of man,' she once told me apologetically.

'What kind of man *is* my father, then?' I asked.

'Too self-confident. Too successful. Too . . . just too, *too*. In every way.'

'I love you,' I said. It was the first time I'd ever said that to her.

36

Here follows the course of a carefree spring day on a Wadden Island:

7.45 Get up. Shower. Wake Bo.

8.03 Go to the bakery. Fry eggs. Set breakfast table with fresh buns, orange juice and strong coffee.

8.28 Eat breakfast.

9.33 Finally finish breakfast. Leave all dirty dishes on the counter.

9.50 Go to the bike-hire place. Pick out a pair of sturdy Dutch two-wheelers.

10.04 Go cycling. Through the fields and along the dyke on the shallows side, to Nes. Gambolling lapwings, hysterical godwits, a flight of wigeons, two Nile geese in a long, straight, grey ditch. 'If you could choose between the Nile and this ditch . . .' 'If you could choose between Amsterdam and Ameland . . .' 'Then I'd still be glad we live in Amsterdam.'

11.28 A coffee shop in Buren. Just when we've found a seat, in come the five young people we saw yesterday on the mudflats. 'See any more seals this morning?' the same boy asks. 'Don't pay any attention to him,' says the same girl – the girl with the black baseball cap. 'Are you staying here in Buren?' 'No, in Hollum.' 'Is that nice, Hollum?' 'Yeah, quite nice.' 'Is there anywhere to go out at night?' 'Ummm ... well, we only got here yesterday.'

12.15 We're ready to leave. 'Bye,' says Bo. 'Ciao.' 'See you,' says the girl with the cap. 'She was flirting with you,' I say when we get outside. 'Ar-min,' Bo sighs.

12.43 Walk across the sand at Het Oerd. Black scoters beyond the breakers. A sick rabbit, waiting for a buzzard or a fox. Waiting for death. Bo finds the skull of a seagull, clean and completely intact. He puts it in his tin.

13.30 Lunch atop a dune. 'What do you think, shall we blow up that production platform?' 'Good idea.'

14.07 Back to the bikes. We head west, on the lee side of the dune. Late-brooding fieldfares. Hoping for a short-eared owl, but all we see is a buzzard, flapping low over the grassland in semi-successful mimicry – semi-successful, because I stop anyway and pull out my binoculars. 'Buzzard,' I say to Bo. 'I thought so.' Show-off, I think. But I say nothing.

14.50 Close to Ballum, a short side-trip to the beach. Dead jellyfish. Sanderlings. Bo finds a skate's egg, I find a right shoe. How does it go again? In England, more left shoes are found on the North Sea Coast; in Holland and Belgium, more right shoes – or was it the other way around? In any case, it had something to do with the current and the specific streamlining of left and right shoes. We agree that, however it went, it had to be the other way around.

15.34 Back on the bikes. We head 'home'.

16.09 In the village we buy a bottle of whisky and a

couple of beers. Plus a copy of *Voetbal International* and *Bild Zeitung*.

16.16 Home. Reading. A drink close at hand. 'Feyenoord disappoints loyal fans'. '*Schadenfreude in Bonn*'.

18.30 'What are we going to eat?' I awake with a start. 'Let's go out.' 'Good idea.' 'Where?' 'Here in the village.' 'Sole Picasso.' 'Something like that. Sea wolf?' 'Mullet.' 'Outstanding.'

19.07 A local restaurant with seascape murals and fishing nets hanging from the ceiling. 'I'd like the Sole Picasso.' 'And I'd like the gurnard in mild mustard sauce. And a carafe of white wine, please.'

That kind of day. The kind of day that in no way prepares you for what the night will bring.

37

If only I hadn't got so drunk.

If only I hadn't got so drunk, I would never have drowned myself in self-pity.

If only I hadn't got so drunk, I would have realized that he was sleeping with his eyes closed.

If only I hadn't got so drunk, I . . .

After dinner and coffee we take a walk through the fields, towards the shallows. To the west, the lighthouse flashes. To the east, a vague glow announces moonrise. Every once in a while the nervous cry of a redshank sounds in the darkness, the suppressed keewee-ee-ee-eet of an alarmed lapwing. We pass a field of sheep that stare at us as we go by, as though we're the first humans they've ever seen. We don't say much.

Bo says, 'It really is quiet.'

I say nothing.

Bo says, 'What are we going to do?'

I say, 'Walk a little. Go drink some coffee.'

We follow the darkened asphalt between two ditches that reflect the night sky. The fresh air is not having its desired effect on me. Instead of perking up, I become sadder at every step. Maybe it's because, in the dark, I have to do without the reassurance of this unchanging landscape. Maybe it's because, in the dark, death is more real than life. Maybe it's because Bo won't match my pace – something that has never bothered me before, but now it does.

We walk back to the village, with a slight detour. The houses wait for us with lighted windows that are inviting and excluding, all at the same time. We go into the first café we find and sit at a table by the window. There aren't many other customers.

'Evening.'

'Good evening.'

A boy with blushing cheeks and an enormous pair of hands takes our order: one coffee, one hot chocolate with whipped cream. I take cognac along with my coffee, Bo takes a glass of water. Just as the boy is putting our steaming cups in front of us, a group of young people comes into the café. It's the two boys and three girls we've seen twice already. It seems they've decided to see for themselves whether Hollum's as nice as Bo said this morning. To judge from the expression on the face of one of the girls, the conclusion is already affirmative – it's the girl with the black baseball cap. As she shuffles past our table, she grants Bo a pearly smile. Even my gloom is lightened by it. Bo mumbles a barely perceptible 'Hello' and begins stirring his hot chocolate vigorously.

I say nothing.

Bo says, 'You think Ellen misses us, a little bit?' He'd asked that at dinner, too.

'She's pleased to be shot of us for a while. Or at least me.' That's what I'd told him at dinner, too.

We drink in silence. The group of five is sitting at

the bar behind us. The girl with the cap has positioned herself in such a way that she can talk to her friends while keeping an eye on Bo. I see her gaze wander regularly to our table.

I don't say anything. I'm thinking. How long have girls been falling for him? I've never noticed it before, and Bo would be the last one to talk about it – if he's even noticed. Oh that terrific, terrible uncertainty of puberty, in which even the most unequivocal feminine signal can never be unequivocal enough. In which every temptation is also cause for alarm, when your self-esteem is as vulnerable as a sandcastle in the surf. Because what one moment seems a probability bordering on certainty may turn out the next to be an absolute impossibility. Because you know nothing, and understand nothing. Or is that an old man talking? Are today's adolescents much wiser than that? I look at Bo and think: no, that uncertainty is of all ages. But I can't be too certain. After all, what do I know about him – except that he is not my son?

'I have to go to the toilet.'

He gets up. The eyes of the girl-with-the-cap flash in his direction. Bo looks around hesitantly. By watching her expression, I can see the exact moment their gazes cross. That smile again. (Chimpanzees also show each other their teeth as a sign of reassurance – unlike many other animals, including dogs. Grinning at a mean dog can have nasty consequences. Not grinning at a mean dog can, too. Smiling at someone you desire is almost always a good first move.) I can't see whether Bo is smiling back, but he shuffles right past her on his way to the toilet. I catch myself envying him. I take a quick swig of my cognac and turn to stare out of the window, even though my view is largely obscured by the reflection in the glass.

Bo is flirting.

Bo isn't a little boy any more.

Oh, what the hell, I'd lost him anyway.

What a ridiculous, pitiful thought!

It's nice for him. That's right, it's nice for him. And what's more, she's a nice girl.

What do you know about it, you old windbag?

Well, a nice girl is a nice girl. That never changes. I still have an eye for that.

But Bo's taste may be different.

Is taste inherited, or is it learned? The fact that men like big tits is biologically determined, the sociobiologists say. Big tits and broad hips. It's been studied. I glance over at the corner of the bar where the girl with the cap is sitting. She's not there any more. Ridiculous of me to wonder about that. I don't even like big tits.

Where is she?

Gone to the toilet, obviously. Is the door of the ladies' in the same alcove as the gents'? Must be. From where I'm sitting, I can't see either of them. Is she waiting for him? I wouldn't have dared to do that, back then. But then, times have changed. Haven't they? No. Monika probably did things like that, too. She lost her virginity when she was thirteen. Thirteen! When she told me that, I'd been speechless. It took me six months to work up the courage to tell her that she was the first.

Thirteen . . . I felt like such an ass. But my inexperience, when I finally dared to confess it, had a remarkable effect on Monika.

'Really?' she asked.

'Really,' I said.

She looked at me questioningly for a while. Then she smiled (that smile, that smile!) and said, 'Then you're a natural.' Whether she really meant it, or whether she was only saying it to make me feel good, I couldn't have cared less; after that, we fucked even more.

'You've got some catching up to do,' Monika said.

'That you saved all that for me,' Monika said.

'How sweet!' Monika said.

And she taught me everything there was to be taught about sex. And after that I taught her what it meant when sex came forth out of true love, because that, she said, was something she'd never experienced before.

That's how we riveted ourselves together.

What God brings together, say the priests and pastors, let no man put asunder. But what man brings together, I say in turn, God cannot put asunder. Not even if he hires a hit-man. Not even if . . . not even then? No, not even then, I tell myself. And I order another cognac. In the hope that I'll keep believing it.

Bo still hasn't come back from the men's room.

38

I have three memories of the last time Monika and I were together on Ameland. The first is linked to the photo on the beach – 'Armin is crazy'. The second has to do with the short-eared owl. We're lying in the spring sun, out of the wind in a pocket of inland dune. Bo is sleeping between us. Monika is chewing on a blade of grass. She has grass in her hair. She's leaning on one elbow, her head resting on her hand. She says, 'What does it mean to you to be the father of my child?'

It was a typical Monika question. 'What do you mean when you say: I love you?' 'What did it feel like the first time you held Bo in your arms?' 'What does "being faithful" mean to you?' For Monika, nothing was to be taken for granted – at least, nothing that had to do with love. Through her, I found out what's most killing for love: the rut.

I think about it. Then I reply, 'That our lives can't be separated any more. That you can no longer say: my life ends here and yours begins there.'

'Do you feel that limits you?'

'Not at all. That the highest goal in life is individual self-realization is a sales pitch from the psychotherapists and pseudo-gurus. The highest goal is to put an end, once and for all, to exclusivist thinking.'

'Excuse me? What's that: "exclusivist thinking"?'

'It's the kind of thinking that draws distinctions and isolates. The kind of thinking that serves as an excellent tool for verifying fact, but which has unfortunately been elevated to a goal in itself. The kind of thinking that forms the greatest obstacle to achieving wisdom.'

'You're shitting through your teeth again, Armin. Could you put that in terms a mere mortal might understand?'

'You're the one who asked,' I splutter. But I've tried that line on her many times before, and she's never fallen for it yet. Not this time, either.

'You know how much I hate all those abstractions. All I asked was whether you minded that Bo meant our lives could no longer be separated. That's a very simple question, isn't it?'

During our first two years together, conversations like this had often led to heated arguments. I took her criticism as out-and-out aggression, and didn't know what I'd done to deserve it. She, in turn, found my abstractions insulting, as though I was consciously trying to belittle her by inflating the simplest questions into philosophical issues. But that afternoon on Ameland, in the early spring sun, we recognized the dangers and both added some water to the wine.

She shooed away an insect that was zooming around her head and said, 'What exactly are you trying to say?'

And I said, 'In order to understand how the body works, it can be very useful to dissect it and study the parts piece by piece. In order to better understand genius and insanity, it can be very helpful to draw a distinction between body and mind. And of course our insight into lightning, rainbows and solar eclipses increased when we stopped seeing them as manifestations of divine emotion. In that sense, it can be quite useful to think in exclusive terms. In terms of either one thing or the other. But the bothersome thing about exclusivist thinking is that, in the long run, it starts seeing itself as the only correct way of thinking – that, after all, is why it's exclusive. And that leads to intellectual paralysis, and even to outright stupidity.'

'For example?'

'For example, take the discussions about what determines who we are: our genes or our environment. Full-blown academic battles have been fought over issues like that, even though it should be clear to everyone from the start that both factors play a part and, what's more, even influence each other. You run into sense-less, all-or-nothing debates like that all the time. About market versus planned economies. About homeopathy versus allopathy. About masculinity versus femininity. About man as calculating egotist versus man as a social creature. About good versus evil.'

'And now back to you and me and Bo.'

She smiles when she says it, the chimpanzee code for 'I mean well'.

I say, 'According to the proponents of exclusivist thinking, people lose their individuality when they bond with others. But I believe that love actually allows people to become more themselves by fusing with another person. Through Bo, you and I are inextricably linked for the rest of our lives. But through that link, I feel freer than I ever did before. The opposite of exclusivist thinking, I believe, lies in the true acceptance of the paradoxical. The key to every bit of wisdom is a paradox.'

And at that very moment a short-eared owl comes in fast and low over the surrounding hedge of buckthorn, swerves and tips its wing when it sees us, and disappears as silently as it came.

'Pure coincidence,' I say, 'but, of course, not without portent.'

And Monika says, 'Pfffff!' and laughs stridently. And I crawl across Bo and push her down in the grass and kiss her until she's quiet.

The third memory has to do with the evening that followed that day. For years I've only dared to think back on that when Ellen was very close. Because Ellen understands. That I had to think about that evening there in that café in Hollum, with Ellen so far away, should have been a warning to me.

39

They come back together. The girl's eyes are glistening even more brightly. You can't see a thing on Bo. The girl goes back to her barstool. Bo comes over to our table, but doesn't sit down. He says, 'I'm going over there.' And he nods back towards the bar. 'Those are the people we met this morning, remember?'

'Sure I do. Have fun.'

I peer at the reflections in the window and try to think about nothing – which doesn't work, which *never* works. When I look up a little later, one of the boys is talking excitedly to Bo. Every once in a while, Bo says something back. The girl-with-the-cap, who's standing just behind him, never takes her eyes off Bo. I order a glass of red wine from the boy with the workman's hands.

'Red wine for the gentleman.'

'Thank you very much.'

Two glasses of red wine later, a man is suddenly standing beside my table.

'Is this chair taken?'

'No, help yourself.'

He's enormous. I slide the table towards me a bit to make room for his stomach. He grins at me. Limpid blue eyes in a face that seems to glow permanently from being out of doors. A dark, not particularly neat beard. Teeth

that seem to indicate a heavy nicotine addiction. As soon
as he's seated he pulls a rumpled pack of dark cigarette
tobacco out of his pocket and begins to roll one.

'Mind if I smoke?'

'Go ahead.'

'Holiday?'

'Three-day weekend.'

'Let me guess: Amsterdam?'

'Good guess.'

'Accent. Clothes. Self-confidence bordering on indifference. I can pick them out in a crowd, I can,
Amsterdammers.'

'Hollum?' I ask.

'Ballum.' He lights his roll-up. Takes a deep drag.
Blows the smoke at the ceiling.

'That your son?' He nods his head back towards the
bar, precisely the way Bo did half an hour ago.

'Yeah.'

'Looks just like you. Same movements. Same self-
confidence bordering on indifference.'

I have to laugh at that.

'What's so funny?'

'One of the girls in that group has her eye on him. And
I don't think he feels awfully self-confident about that.'
(All the other things I could say, about resemblances
between people who aren't related, and what that says
about the influence of environment and genes, all those
things I don't say.)

He turns his huge body towards the bar. It makes the
table shake. The wine slops over the rim of my glass. Just
to be safe, I pick up the glass. He sits there examining

the group of young people for a while. I look along with him.

Bo is still talking to the same boy. That is to say, the boy is talking at Bo, gesturing excitedly, and Bo says something back on occasion. But now when he says something he no longer looks at the boy, but at the girl-with-the-cap. And she answers him with her eyes, and every once in a while with her mouth. And suddenly it seems to dawn on the boy what is happening right before his eyes. He takes a little step back. Looks at the girl. Looks at Bo, who's saying something to her at that very moment. Then he turns demonstratively to the girl, but she doesn't even glance at him. She's still looking at Bo. And Bo keeps talking imperturbably. The boy tries again to take over the conversation, but again it doesn't work. Then he turns abruptly and orders something from the barman.

The man across from me at the table turns back. The table shakes again. The wineglass is suspended safely between my fingers.

'Puppy love,' he says, so loudly that I'm afraid Bo will hear it. (But Bo doesn't react.)

'That'll be kissing in the dark. And touchy-feely. Ha ha ha!'

I laugh along with him, but not entirely with conviction. You're turning into a grouchy old shit, I think to myself. But I say, 'Can I buy you a drink?' And he says I can.

Bas is the name of my table companion and drinking partner. And he's no fisherman, no farmer, no roughneck, no ship's pilot, no beachcomber, no publican and no cook. Bas is a biologist. He's studying the effects of cockle-fishing on eider ducks in the Wadden Shallows. The effects are disastrous. Tens of thousands of birds have died of starvation in the last few years; the result of the new, intensive fishing methods, as practised particularly by the fleet from Dutch Zealand that frequents the shallows.

'For the first time in years,' Bas says, the foam of a third beer in his beard, 'my work has gained me a certain popularity on the island. Conservationists aren't loved here. The islanders often feel that the birds are considered more important than they are. And that hurts. I can understand that. But now that the Zealanders are to blame, of course, that's all changed. A bunch of foreigners ripping up the sea floor, that's the bloody limit.' His laugh is infectious, his enthusiasm is too. He talks about the eider ducks as though they were the crown of creation.

'A grown male eider in his Sunday best can still bring tears to my eyes,' he says. 'Even after all these years. I'm not a poet, unfortunately, but if I were I'd write an ode to the eider drake. That clownish black and white, alongside those soft pastels. I feel about eider drakes the way I do about pretty women. When I see a really pretty woman, I tend to think: how can she belong to the same species as a fat, ugly lummox like me? And when I see those dark, stodgy female eiders beside a beautiful drake with that almost tropical plumage, I also wonder how in the world that can be. If you ask me, God's a big practical joker.'

And he laughs that robust laugh and turns around so

he can see Bo and the girl-with-the-cap, who only have eyes for each other. (They're both drinking red port – I've never seen Bo drink that before!)

Talking to Bas with the belly and the beard and the beer has dispelled my sombre mood, so I decide to change from red wine to something more cheerful. I order a double whisky on the rocks.

'Or, on second thoughts, hold the rocks.'

Bas joins me.

'Don't mean to pry,' he says when our drinks arrive, 'but where's the missus?'

'The missus is . . .' I'm about to say 'dead'. But I'm afraid to fall back into that mire of melancholy and self-pity. 'At home, in Amsterdam. It was time for the men to go off on their own.'

'Very good,' Bas says. 'A boys' day out. I bet that son of yours . . . what's his name again? Bo, right, Bo . . . I bet Bo wouldn't feel nearly as comfortable with that girl over there if he knew his mother was sitting here.'

And suddenly I see Monika across from me at the table. With a glass of red wine in her hand, and her red hair all mussed from cycling into the wind. Didn't we once sit here, here in this same café, at this very table? Could be. She was wearing an apple-green jacket. With a purple scarf. She was the liveliest-looking thing on the island. And she knew it. That semi-ironic smile she turned on the world was her way of saying, 'That's right, take a good look, this is what became of that ugly little redhead with freckles, the one you all teased as a child. Now you're sorry, now you'd like to get to know me, now you want to touch me, but it's too late. I don't need you any more. I'm perfectly happy without you. I have a man I love who loves me, and me alone. And I have a child I cry with and laugh with. And all of us laugh at you. The three of us against the rest of the world. And we can win with our hands in our pockets.'

That's how Monika looked at the world, in the spring of 1987.

Why did God have to put a contract out on that?

I knock back my whisky in one go. Bas looks at me in amazement. But he says nothing. A boys' day out.

I remember Bo coming over to me at a certain point.

'I'm going with them. Somewhere else.'

'Good. Have fun.'

Bas and I laughed and drank and talked. He told me a hilarious story about a drunken cockle fisher, but I've forgotten the punchline. Or maybe there wasn't any punchline. He told me about his father, who'd worked on ships plying the coast of Scandinavia. About storms on the Kattegat and the Sont. About perfumed letters from Sweden that had driven his mother to despair. He talked about crates of expensive wine he'd found on the beach as a child. And about a bloated corpse that had suddenly popped up in the surf a few years ago, in the middle of a group of children at play. He told island stories. And I listened. And finally he asked me about life in Amsterdam. And I returned to my years as a drunk, which were suddenly right there before my eyes (the way drunken goldfish remember the tricks they learned under the influence).

I said, 'One rainy October night I was walking through the red-light district. It must have been about four or five in the morning. Things were getting quiet. I was carrying Bo on my back, and I was looking at the women sitting at their windows and they were looking at me. One of the women tapped on the window and gestured to me, and I thought: out here it's cold and wet, and in there I bet it's nice and warm. I stuck my hand in my pocket and found some banknotes and, even though I didn't know whether they were tens or hundreds, I still walked over to the door. The woman opened the door for us and I stepped inside and put Bo on the only chair in the room and she closed the curtains and asked me my name. I thought that was sweet of her, to want me to have a name. I'd been talking to people all night, in bars and out on the street, and no one had asked me my name. The woman was German; she had a heavy accent. Andrea was her name. At least that's what she called herself. She thought Armin and Bo sounded German, and I let her think that. She asked Bo if he wanted to take off his coat, but he was asleep. So I said, "Bo sleeps with his eyes open." At first she didn't believe me. She went over and stood in front of him, in her black negligée, and she waved her carefully manicured fingers in front of his face. He didn't react. Then she believed me. "Why does he do that?" she asked. "Because of a nightmare," I said. "*Arme Jungen.*" We sat down on the bed, Andrea and I. "Where is his *Mutter*?" she asked. "She's dead," I said.' And then I explained to Bas, 'Bo's mother died ten years ago.'

Bas nodded, as though it were completely normal that

the mother who had just been at home in Amsterdam was now suddenly ten years dead. And, in fact, it was. People not telling the truth about things like that is the most normal thing in the world.

'That's why I drank so much back then,' I said. 'That's why I was wandering with my son through the red-light district at five in the morning.'

The barman brought us more beer. Apparently we were no longer drinking whisky.

'We sat on that bed for a long time,' I went on. 'She was a wonderful girl. She told me she had a daughter almost Bo's age. I asked about the first words she'd taught her child. "*Mein Vati ist ein Arschloch*," she said. Her daughter's name was Maria. She hoped Maria would remain a virgin all her life. I gave her two hundred guilders. But when we got home and I was undressing Bo for bed, I found the money. She'd tucked it into his clothes. That's the only time I've ever visited a whore.'

When we'd finished our beer, I got up to leave.

'Be careful,' Bas said.

And I said, 'We've got a house just around the corner. I'll be all right.' But it took me a long time to find it.

Bo wasn't there.

40

I woke up with a splitting headache. My tongue was leather and my stomach felt like a reactor vat that was about to explode. I was sitting in a chair in the living room of the little house. Outside, it was turning light. On the fence in front of the house was a blackbird. *Chuuk-chuuk-chuuk-chuuk*, said the blackbird. I walked into the kitchen and filled a tall cocktail glass with water. Three times. Then I went back to my chair, picked the bottle of whisky off the floor and took two hefty swigs.

It didn't help.

I went to the toilet and pissed and drank more water. Then I went to the room with the double bed, opened the door and ... Lying in the bed were Bo and the girl-with-the-cap. Without the cap. The cap was lying on the floor, on top of her other clothes. She was wearing a T-shirt. One of Bo's. Bo was wearing a T-shirt, too. It wasn't a shocking sight in any way, more romantic, innocent even. He was asleep. She was asleep. Her arm was lying across him. I closed the door again and sat down in my chair. I poured another glass of whisky and wondered why my hands were shaking so badly.

I remember seeing the girl walk through the house that morning in her underpants and that T-shirt of Bo's.

I remember Bo making coffee. Later there was a mug of cold coffee beside my chair. I remember that I wanted to pour myself another glass of whisky to get rid of the headache. But the whisky was finished. Fortunately, there was still a bottle of beer.

I went back into the room with the double bed. The room was empty. The bed wasn't made. I fell right onto my back. The beer sloshed out of the bottle. What was left of it I drank at one go. I felt the cold liquid running down my chin and neck. I closed my eyes. The world spun. I thought about Monika. I thought about Ellen, who I could never give the thing she wanted most of all. I thought about my son who wasn't my son, and who dared to do things at fourteen that I'd dared only when I was twenty. And I thought: he gets that from his father. And then I thought about Niko Neerinckx and about Anke. And I cursed myself for not fucking her. For still being a coward, only half a man. And I tried to imagine how she'd look without clothes, how I'd tear the clothes off her body, how she'd give herself to me, how she would struggle fruitlessly. I wanted to get an erection. An erection because of *her*. But I was too drunk for that.

I rolled onto my stomach and buried my face in the pillow. The pillow smelled of girl. I cried.

'Armin! Armin! What are you doing here? This is *my* bed! Fuck off, Armin! You're drunk! You puked! Pig! Armin!'

Bo is yanking on my shoulder. Screaming in my ear. I roll over. The world spins back the other way. Bo is

hanging in the air, upside down. Despite his predica-
ment, it seems he's able to hit me. He strikes me square
in the face, with the flat of his hand. I hear the smack.
Bo revolves a hundred and eighty degrees and falls into
place. The walls of the room come flying in on me.

'What's wrong?' I shout. But I can't hear myself.

Apparently Bo can't hear me, either. 'Go to your own
room, you pig!' he shouts.

I try to sit up. Something is sticking to my cheek. I
wipe my hand across my face. There's my hand, floating
in space. Now there's something sticking to my fingers.
Something yellow. I look at the spot where I was just
lying. I feel a wave of gall roll up into my gullet. The
pillow is covered in vomit.

'Jesus.'

'Yeah, Jesus, yeah!' Bo screams. Why is he screaming
like that? Is he afraid I can't hear him? And why did he
hit me? He hit me! The son of a bitch! The bastard!

'What the fuck do you think you're doing?' Now
there's sound coming out of my mouth. It scrapes and
rasps in my throat, but I don't care. He's going to hear
me. 'Who do you think are? Smack me around because I
puked in your little love nest, hey? Embarrassed in front
of the girl, is that it? Because your father's a drunk! Well,
pal, let me put your mind at ease. I'm not your father! Do
you hear that? You hear that? I'm not your father! Your
father is some sneaky little skirt-chaser from Haarlem
who couldn't keep his hands off your mother. That's
a surprise, isn't it! He was probably fucking little girls
when he was fourteen, too!'

He'd taken three steps back, Bo. He'd gone all pale

while I was ranting and raving at him. 'What kind of bullshit is that?' he'd shouted. And then he'd suddenly jumped on me. As hard as a boy could, he'd hit me. I felt his fists against my chest, in my face, against my ears. I kept my eyes closed and all the strength ran out of me.

It had been said. It had finally been said.

41

On the front page of the NRC *Handelsblad* of 24 March 1983 is a photo of a photo. In the first frame you see the American president, Ronald Reagan. In one hand the president has a pile of papers. With the other he's pointing at something beyond the view of the photographer, and therefore beyond that of the reader as well. Right above the pointing hand is the second photo, on a tripod, in a black frame. What that photo shows is a number of vague white lines against a grey background. In bold, black letters, the caption explains: 'Soviet MiGs, Western Cuba.' It's an espionage photo of a military installation on Fidel Castro's sugar island.

The day Bo was born, the Cold War entered a new phase. Ronald Reagan had just launched his Star Wars programme. Bo was born in a world that no longer exists.

I look at the photo, and at the photo within the photo, in my parents' living room. Amazingly, they saved a newspaper from the day my son was born. And that's not all. I found the paper in a box that turned out to be full of Bo souvenirs. Photographs. Drawings. A report card. An exercise book. Where did they get all this?

I show the photos to Dees, who's helping me clear the house.

Bo as a baby, nursing at Monika's breast.

Bo's first school picture: taken at the day-care centre.

Bo on my mother's lap.

Bo holding my father's hand at the zoo.

Bo's face smeared with chocolate pudding.

Bo wearing clothes covered in mud and sand.

'Did you know that?' Dees asks. 'Did you know they had all this?'

'No, I've never seen it before.'

We spread the newspaper on the floor. 'Liberals threaten with crisis over spending cuts.' How thrilling. 'Man with artificial heart dies.' Poor sod. ('Barney Clark, the first man to live with an artificial heart, died yesterday in Salt Lake City, the hospital reported. Clark lived for 112 days with a heart made of plastic and aluminium.') 'Flimsy ball opens National Book Week.' 'Belgium says no to more Dutch waste.' '$500 million loan to Iraq.' ('Iraq has been granted an inter-national loan for the sum of $500 million. The loan was underwritten by thirty-four major international banks, including one of America's biggest financial institutions, Chase Manhattan. This bank, whose board of directors maintains close relationships with a number of top Arab officials, was said to have lobbied strongly for American participation in the project.' What do you know about that?) And, at 7 p.m., Holland 1 kicked off prime time with *Like Father, Like Daughter*, while at 8.10 p.m. the Avro broadcasting company on Holland 2 struck back with *What's My Line?* O, beautiful, bourgeois Holland in which Bo produced his first dirty nappy!

'I told him,' I say without further introduction.

'What? Who?'

'Bo. That I'm not his father.'

'You're crazy.'

'I was drunk, mostly. He'd been hitting me. Because I puked on the pillow where he'd kissed his first girl. Or perhaps even fucked her.'

'What? What, what the hell?'

He closes the paper angrily. Sits down in a chair. 'Tell me again. Preferably in some logical order.'

So I tell him. About the girl-with-the-cap on the mudflats. And how we ran into her again that evening in the bar. And about Bas with his belly and his beard and his beer. And about the whisky. And the double bed. And about how Bo slapped me. And what I said then. And what Bo did then.

'Shit!' Dees says. 'Shit, man! Goddamn, shit!'

I sit on the floor, pick up the photos of Bo and put them back in the box.

Glad my father doesn't have to hear all this.

Good thing he can't see me now.

His failure of a son.

Dees stares at me with dark eyes. I get up. Walk to the window.

'Just say it,' I say.

'Shithead.'

'Yeah.'

'Unbelievable shithead.'

'Yeah.'

The room is silent for a long time. Outside a woman walks past with an ugly little dog on a ridiculously long leash. I think about the neighbour, Mr Bruggeman, and about Boris. I haven't seen them today. Maybe he's dead, I think. Justice at last.

Dees sighs. 'How's Bo taking it?'

'No idea. Not too well, I think. When he'd finished hitting me he jumped off the bed and walked out of the house without a word. I fell asleep. When I woke up that evening, he still wasn't back. I cleaned the bed. Made some food. Then I tried to read a book, but I couldn't. About one o'clock he came back. He didn't say anything. Went straight to his room. The next morning I woke him up, with a fresh croissant and orange juice. I said we needed to talk. I said I understood that he was angry and upset. And that he needed to give it time. That he should ask me to explain whenever he was ready to hear it. He didn't ask me anything all day. Early that afternoon we took the boat back, half a day earlier than we'd planned. We drove all the way home without a word. It was the longest, most horrible silence since Monika stopped talking.

'Christ almighty,' Dees says.

'Yeah.'

'How did Ellen react?'

'Ellen doesn't know yet. She wasn't there when we got home. She hadn't been expecting us yet. When she got home that evening, Bo was already in bed. She asked how it had been and I said, "Good." And she asked, "Is something wrong?" I wasn't looking too happy, of course. But I said, "No, I'm just really tired. Bo is too.

He's gone to bed already." In bed I crawled right up against her. She was restless, couldn't get to sleep. She knows something's wrong. But this morning I left early, before she'd have a chance to ask me about it.'

Another long silence between Dees and me.

He takes a couple of deep breaths, as if he's about to say something. But he says nothing. Finally, I'm the one who breaks the silence.

'You know what's the weirdest thing of all? When Bo and that girl were sleeping in that big bed, he had his eyes closed. I swear to God. But at that moment it just didn't sink in. That's how drunk I was.'

Dees laughs. But not with a lot of feeling.

Two hours later.

We've filled six big cardboard boxes with things I want to save. The Bo souvenirs. Classical records. Lots of Beethoven. I don't like Beethoven. Lots of Brahms. I don't like Brahms. But they're records my mother cried to. And that my father listened to during the last days of his life. I can't just leave them here for Second-Hand Rose. Three boxes, full of books. Old children's books. My mother's Bible. My father's shelf of Dutch classics. Louis Couperus. Frederik van Eeden. Arthur van Schendel. Vestdijk, of course. Nine times Vestdijk. I also found the religious book the neighbour had returned to the shelf, the last book my father ever read. The neighbour had given it a place next to Vestdijk's *The Last Days of Pilate*, which I thought was a nice gesture. To my amazement, it turned out to be the same book I'd found among Monika's books ten years ago, *The Secret Teachings of Jesus of Nazareth*, including 'The Revelations of Jacob', 'The Gospel of Thomas' and 'The Gospel of Philip'.

The way everything that goes by keeps coming back.

I put the book in with my mother's Bible, because my mother must have been the one who bought it – and maybe even gave it to Monika. (Monika wasn't religious, but my mother always said you could tell by looking her that she came from the Catholic south. And she definitely meant that as a compliment.)

Once the last box is filled, Mr Bruggeman comes over with Boris, just to take a look and have a talk. The dog runs excitedly through the house. And Mr Bruggeman talks and talks and talks.

'Two days ago,' he says, 'I woke up suddenly in the middle of the night. I heard voices and someone crashing around. It sounded like two people having a fight – a man and a woman. I could have sworn it was coming from this house. But of course that's impossible. No, that's impossible. I lay there listening to it, my heart pounding. But no matter how hard I tried, I couldn't make out a word they were saying. I got up and turned on a light. I thought: maybe it's only in my head. But at one point it got so bad that Boris started barking. Then I put on my dressing-gown and went outside to see if the lights were on at the neighbours' across the street. But it was all dark. And outside I didn't hear it any more, the fighting. Inside, Boris just kept barking. When he eventually stopped, it was quiet everywhere. The rest of the night, I didn't sleep a wink.'

Dees said, 'Sometimes at night it's hard to tell where sounds are coming from.'

'Yeah,' Mr Bruggeman said. 'Yeah, sure.'

'My father's wine collection,' I say to him, 'is for you.'

He tries to refuse. But not for long.

After he's gone I take one last turn through the house, to be sure I didn't miss anything. Dees starts taking the boxes out to the car. Everything we leave behind now goes to Second-Hand Rose. The bookcase. The coffee table. The leather sofa. The bed. The bed, too? Yes, the bed, too.

I lean against the doorpost in the bedroom and try to imagine my parents, together in that bed, which now looks bare and inhospitable without sheets or blankets. Two years ago they slept here together for the last time. Did they know, that night before the day my mother went into hospital, that it was the last time? Did they talk about it, he in one of his many pairs of striped pyjamas (they too, are going to Second-Hand Rose), she in a modest nightgown? (I didn't find any of my mother's clothes, not a single scarf, not one pair of forgotten gloves, nothing. What my father did with them, I have no idea.) I yank myself out of my reverie and bend over to take a last look under the bed – an old holiday habit. And I see something under it. A little box I must have missed before. I pull it out. It's made of tropical hardwood, mahogany inlaid with ebony and mother-of-pearl. I sit on the edge of the bed and open it. Letters. Postcards. From my father to my mother. From my mother to my father. A picture postcard from

Brittany, from Monika and me. A letter I wrote to my mother when she was already ill. Downstairs I hear a door slam. I have to help Dees. This will have to wait until a moment when I'm feeling up to it. A moment when Ellen is around, to hold me tight if it seems as if I'm about to fall off the world. Absentmindedly, I let the cards and letters glide through my hands. Then a little envelope catches my eye. 'COR' is written on it, in block letters. My father's nickname. Nothing else. The envelope has been torn open at the side. I shake out the piece of paper. It's a note, with a brief message. Written in a feminine hand, it reads: 'I'm pregnant. M.'

What's the best way to take a blow? Roll with it. Make sure you don't receive the full impact at once.

'I'm pregnant. M.'

Monika wrote my father a letter to tell him she was pregnant. That's all.

It looks like she delivered the letter in person, because there's no address on the envelope, no stamp. That's all.

What could that mean?

That . . . can . . . mean . . . only . . . one . . . thing.

Can't it?

One thing.

I try to stuff the letter back into the envelope. But my hands are shaking too badly. I put it back on the pile, along with the envelope. I close the box. Walk down the stairs.

'What's that?' Dees asks.

'Some letters and postcards.'

Together we carried the last boxes to the car. After a lot of juggling, we finally got them all in. The little wooden box of letters I put on the floor behind the passenger seat. I remember looking in the mirror as we pulled away. In a little rectangular frame, I saw my parents' house slide past as I turned the car and drove out of the street. For the last time through the old town centre with its two gigantic churches, its little bridges across the Gein. 'Abcoude – the old ABC', as my father used to say. A stupid joke, but suddenly it made me roar with laughter.

Dees didn't react. Dees was still mad at me. Or deeply disappointed in me, at the very least. I thought: if you only knew what I've just found out. But I said nothing. We drove up onto the A2 and it took all the energy I had not to yank the wheel at a hundred and twenty and throw the car into the guardrail.

After I've dropped Dees at his house ('Let me know how it goes,' he says, 'and hang in there.'), I drive on to the Amsterdamse Bos. I don't want to go home yet, can't go home yet.

I'm pregnant. M.

What else could it mean but . . . but *that*! The words still don't want to come. I can't even tell myself what I'm thinking. What I know.

I park the car on the lot at the start of the old rowing course, where years ago two Amsterdam patrolmen encountered a suspicious canary-yellow Renault 5. I walk into the woods. From far away I hear the plaintive mewing of the peacocks at the farm that marks the border between the woods and the old pastureland. Just past the farm I turn left, cross a little wooden bridge and enter the swampy territory of the nightingales. It's a cold day, late April, and except for the monotone call of a chiffchaff, no birds are singing. Maybe the nightingales haven't arrived yet. They're one of the last migratory birds to return from the south. When the nightingales sing, it's not spring that's returning, it's the summer.

The water of the Ringvaart is black and restless. Gusts of wind blow the waves in every direction. Peeping loudly, its head held low above the water, a coot swims towards a foolish, brightly coloured duck. When it arrives within a few metres of the city slicker, it goes into a sprint. Its webbed feet spatter across the surface and it flaps its wings hard, making the water splash all around. The duck flies away, protesting loudly. The coot swims around the spot it just conquered from the intruder, as if to make sure the duck really has left, the danger really is over. (What danger? Why do coots see all other birds as a threat? They're completely paranoid. But maybe that's why they do so well in the city.)

I decide to walk along the shore of the Nieuwe Meer, and then straight across the fields, back to the woods and the rowing course. Actually, I decide nothing at all. It's what happens to me. I'm walked to the shore of the lake and then directed to the right, along the narrow path through the fields. I see the farm rising up amid the fresh green grass. I see it go past. I come back to the car and am put behind the wheel and the engine is started and the car begins to drive and someone steers me safely through traffic, along the ring road, back home. I'm parallel-parked without a hitch.

When I'm standing at the front door with the key in my hand, it flashes through my mind for a moment: now what? But I don't wait for an answer to that question. There is no answer. The door opens. The stairs take me up. Another door opens, and another. I stand in the living room of my own house – the safest place on earth. Here the sacks of coffee once lay piled to the ceiling. Now there are bookcases and a table, chairs and a sofa. Sitting on the sofa are Ellen and Bo. Sitting on the sofa is the son of my father.

42

You can get used to anything, even to what you don't see coming.

Ellen and Bo have both been crying. Red eyes. Streaks down their faces. Hair mussed. But now they're laughing. Bo says, 'It's so insane!' I stand in the doorway and look at them. It takes a moment before he realizes I'm there. He stops laughing right away.

'Hello,' I say awkwardly.

Bo says nothing.

Ellen gets up, comes over to me, throws her arms around me and hugs me. 'How did it go at your father's?'

'It was difficult.'

'You'd better sit down, Armin.'

I plop down in a chair, with the feeling I'll never get up again.

'You want some coffee?'

I want some coffee.

Bo stares at the table. On the table is an envelope. On the envelope is written, 'For Bo.' I recognize the handwriting immediately. It's the same handwriting that was on the little envelope in the box of letters.

Oh God!

Ellen comes in with the coffee. She puts a cup on the table in front of me. Right next to the envelope. That neat, even handwriting, where did she ever get that, anyway? It seems so contrary to who she was – who she turns out to have been.

I wait.

It's quiet in the room. Ellen stirs her coffee. Bo sighs.

'Bo told me what happened,' Ellen says.

I say nothing and stare at the envelope.

'That letter,' Ellen says, 'was once given to me by Monika. If Bo ever needed to know what happened. He needed to know.'

Bo leans forward and picks up the envelope, hands it to me. I look him in the eye for a moment. I look at Ellen, but Ellen is looking at the coffee cup in her hand. I take the letter out of the envelope and read. I don't get any further than the fifth line. Then the letter falls out of my hand. I close my eyes and wait. Nothing comes.

The first lines of the letter read:

Dear Bo,

As I'm writing this, I'm looking at you. You're playing with some plastic thing, and I don't know where you got it. I'm looking at you and thinking: I don't have to write this letter, because you look like your father, just the way your father looks like his father. And how that came to be no one ever has to know. It's a secret between me and the man you'll call your grandfather – and it would be better for everyone if things always stayed that way. But God knows what's good for people usually doesn't happen.

I look really long, really hard at the tip of my left shoe. There's a bit of mud on it, and sticking to that mud is a little feather. I try to tell from looking at it what kind of bird it came from, but it's a rather nondescript thing. Grey. Or dirty-white. When I've stared at the feather long enough, I look at Bo. But Bo has his own feather to stare at. I say, 'So now you know, too.'

He looks up at me. Puzzlement in his eyes. His eyes move to Ellen for support.

'Too?' Ellen asks.

'Yeah,' I say. 'At my father's. I found another letter from Monika.'

I take a sip of coffee.

'So you've known about it all these years?' I ask her. But it doesn't sound like a question. It sounds more like an acceptance.

'Yeah.'

I fold the letter, put it back in the envelope and hand it to Bo. I get up. All my muscles hurt.

'Where are you going?' Ellen asks.

'Out. For a walk.'

'Then I'm going with you.'

I feel like protesting, but I don't have the energy.

43

This was written by Philip the Evangelist: 'When the pearl is cast down into the mud, it does not become greatly despised, nor if it is anointed with balsam oil will it become more precious. But it always has value in the eyes of its owner.'

My mother underlined those words. Just as she underlined the verse about the philanderer which I, in my ignorance, once read aloud to my father's son (my brother!) from the book that belonged to his father's one-time beloved, my beloved Monika. My mother must have known about it all those years. 'Maybe I didn't love him enough. And later on I couldn't any more.' What is that? Why do so many women blame themselves when their husband is unfaithful? I'm prepared to take anything into consideration if it helps me understand what happened, but not that it could be my fault. Did my mother find the note Monika wrote to my father? And did she know right away – the way I knew? Did my father know that my mother knew, or did he only find out when he read the Gospel of Philip and saw the verses that had been underlined. ('The children a woman bears resemble the one she loves. If that is her husband, they resemble her husband. If that is a philanderer, they will resemble that philanderer.' The words that were too much for my father's heart. I should have them carved on a plaque.)

I think about what Bas, the big-bellied, bearded biologist said to me in that café on Ameland: 'God is a big practical joker.' But I don't laugh.

Hundreds of questions have been answered, but thousands of new ones have taken their place. The more I know, the more I realize that I know nothing.

What I know now is how it went, more or less. According to Ellen.

It started with a flash of lightning. ('That's worse than Hollywood,' I said to Ellen. 'Life *is* worse than Hollywood,' she replied.)

My father and Monika had been working in the house on the Ceintuurbaan. My father had plastered a wall, while Monika painted the bedroom ceiling. When she was finished she'd taken a shower, to get the whitewash out of her hair. After that my father took a shower while Monika made tea and sandwiches. It was already late in the afternoon, but they hadn't eaten lunch yet, that's how hard they'd been working. While they were sitting at the improvised kitchen table (a door on sawhorses, with three Ikea folding chairs around it), it had suddenly grown dark outside. Within a few moments, thick summer torrents of rain were washing down from the sky. Monika went and stood in front of the open window. How often had I seen her do that? She had this childlike fascination with heavy rain and thunderstorms. She'd stand there, looking out with big eyes, a smile on her pale face that the strange light of electrical storms made even paler. What I used to do, and what my father must have done as well, was stand behind her, close behind her. And then she'd sort of fall back slowly. Then she'd lean against my chest. Then her red hair would prickle my face. And if the clouds were torn apart by a stroke of lightning, and if the thunder made the windows rattle in their frames, she would lay her head against my shoulder and look up at me. And I always thought: she has the most beautiful, sensual eyes I've ever seen. Did my father think that, too?

'According to Monika,' Ellen said, 'lightning suddenly struck close by. She was startled by the explosion and automatically took a step back. She bumped up against your father, and your father put his arms around her to keep her from falling.' There Ellen had stopped.

'And then?' I asked.

'Do you really want to know?'

'Yes, I really want to know.' Although of course I would rather have known nothing at all.

'Monika said there had been this tension between your father and her for days. That she'd felt this desire that she didn't want to feel, wouldn't allow herself to feel, but it had kept growing stronger. The moment he put his arms around her, it was as though a hole was knocked in the dyke she'd been hiding her feelings behind. That's how she described it.'

Again, Ellen stopped talking. And again I asked her to go on. To tell me everything that she knew and that I didn't want to know, but had to know.

'Monika turned around and kissed your father. He said she shouldn't do that. But he kissed her back . . . And . . . well, yeah. Then they did it.'

'Straight from kissing to fucking?'

'Well, not straight away. But . . . quickly.'

'But . . . but, where? There wasn't . . . there was nothing in that house to make it . . . well, I mean, comfortable.'

'No.'

'On the floor?'

'No.'

'Standing up?'

'. . .'

'Christ, no! My father?' I think I laughed then. For a second. We were walking along the IJ, not far from our house. A cormorant flew by and I remember how its black silhouette slowly dissolved in the tears welling up in my eyes. I sat down on the ground, on the cold, wet asphalt. And I thought: I'm never getting up again. This is it. It's finished. But Ellen hunched down beside me and hugged me and caressed me and pulled me against her. We sat there together like that, while evening fell and the blackbirds started singing and the chill slowly drew up into my bones. And if Ellen hadn't helped me to my feet, if Ellen hadn't said that we had to get home, to Bo, to the present, I'd be sitting there still. I would have died there of a broken heart, like the tragic hero in some nineteenth-century novel.

That's what I would have wanted, but Ellen didn't want that.

This, too, Philip the Evangelist wrote: 'Ignorance is a slave. Knowledge is freedom. If we know the truth, we shall find the fruits of the truth within us.' It's a verse my mother didn't underline. Monika didn't either.

'Did she have an orgasm?'

'Armin!'

'I have to know. *You* know, I know that for sure. And I can't stand thinking that you know more than I do.'

'Yeah.'

'Was she sorry?'

'Yes. No. She was when it turned out she was pregnant. And she felt guilty towards the child, even before it was born.'

'Why did she tell you?'

'Because she had to talk to someone. Because she felt like she was going crazy.'

'Why didn't she leave a letter for me?'

'She left me behind for you, didn't she?'

'Was she in love with my father?'

'No.'

'Was he in love with her?'

'I don't think so.'

'Did she like it?'

'Armin!'

'. . .'

'I think so.'

'You *think* so?'

'Yes. Yes, she liked it.'

'Christ almighty.'

'Please stop this, Armin.'

'Did she only feel guilty towards Bo? Not towards me?'

'No. Yes, also towards you.'

'Did she say that, or are you saying that to make me feel good?'

'No, of course not. Of course she felt guilty. What do you think?'

'What do I think? You don't want to know what I think. I don't even want to know that.'

'She felt terribly guilty.'

'But you just said she wasn't sorry about it.'

'No. Being sorry is something else. Being sorry you feel on your own. Guilt you get from other people.'

'Oh, that's easy, isn't it? So she got her guilt from me!'

'You don't understand.'

'No, I don't understand.'

'I understand that.'

'Oh, thanks a lot.'

I'm taking my rage out on Ellen. My grief. My sorrow. My frustration.

As if she asked for this. Wait, she did ask for this! She lied to me! I knew she knew about it. I knew, but she kept denying it. Now she has to pay for those lies.

What a crock of shit! What a heartless crock of shit. As if she had any choice. As if I would have done any different in her situation. Would I have done any different in her situation? Would I have done any different in Monika's situation?

How warm Ellen's bed had been that cold winter night, when Monika was at home being pregnant from a man she – with her bare arse against the wall – had fucked only once.

Just one time.

'Did you know about it then?'

'Did I know what when?'

'When we did it, that one time, did you already know about Monika and my father?'

'No.' She's quiet for a while. Then she says, 'I rang her the next day. Feeling guilty, I guess. I asked how she was doing. Not too well, she said. I asked whether she wanted me to come over. She did. Come tomorrow, she said. You were at the publishing house that day. That's when she told me. I could have told her that she didn't have to feel so guilty. That she wasn't the only one. That sometimes we all do things we'd have been better off not doing, but that we don't feel sorry about. I could have told her all that. But I didn't. I didn't dare.'

I look at her. She lowers her eyes. I'm not angry any more. I'm not anything any more. Not a father. Not a son. Not a beloved. Not a friend. Nothing. I've ceased to exist. I have to reinvent myself.

Is that what the evangelist meant by the truth making you free?

44

Bo is sleeping with his eyes closed. I can hardly believe it, but it's true. I sit on the edge of his bed and listen to his breathing. The pause between exhale and inhale, that's the loveliest moment of all. Because then, for a fraction, life stands still.

So is that what I want? To make life stand still? Yes. That's what I want.

Statistically speaking, Bo and I probably share a quarter of our genes, although that percentage may be higher, or even a lot lower – that's the rotten thing about average values: as an individual, you never know how they apply to you. (But try telling that to an insurance agent.) That Bo has the line of my jaw is therefore probably no coincidence. That his feet are different sizes, just like mine, probably isn't, either. According to the sociobiologists, now that I know about our blood relationship I will be able to love him more. Although only half as much as when I thought he was my own child, because father and child share half their genes on the average – in other words, twice as many as half-brothers.

This dramatic insight into the relationship between blood ties and love was given us by a certain William Hamilton, who in 1964 published an article in the

Journal of Theoretical Biology with the title 'The Evolution of Social Behaviour'. Hamilton's article was seen by many as the most important breakthrough in evolutionary theory since Gregor Mendel's discovery of the hereditary characteristics of the pea. Before Hamilton, Darwin's theory could be used only to explain egocentricity – social behaviour did not fit within the theory, and was therefore an unpopular field of research for biologists. The only problem was that one could not deny that social behaviour existed, in both animals and humans. Hamilton was the first to provide an evolutionist's explanation of such behaviour.

In short, Hamilton's insight was this: social behaviour can provide an evolutionary advantage when it benefits direct blood relations. The quantity of genes shared by the blood relations is therefore the determining factor. From a genetic point of view, the closer the kinship, the greater the advantage of social behaviour over selfishness. Egocentric genes can therefore be served by altruistic individuals.

'There's only one problem with Hamilton's theory.' It was Dees, of course, who brought this up. 'It's a snake biting its own tail. He proves what must be proven on the basis of the presupposition that evolutionary theory is correct, and from the standpoint that there *is* such a thing as social behaviour.'

But this time I didn't feel like letting him get away with it so easily. 'You could,' I said, 'develop a hypothesis on the basis of Hamilton's theory. For example, that humans or animals will be more egoistical in proportion to the extent that other individuals in an experiment are more distantly related. In general, experiments seem to support that hypothesis.'

'All well and good,' Dees countered, 'but the only thing that proves is that the parson always christens his own child first – and that, to put it mildly, is not exactly a scientific breakthrough. If Hamilton is right, there should be a direct relationship between a given gene, or at most a pair of genes, and the social behaviour shown. What's more, we're supposed to believe that our genes contain information somewhere that enables us – *unconsciously!* – to distinguish between close relatives and those three or four times removed. But then you may as well believe in God, or in little green men from outer space.'

I had to admit that I could bring no reasonable argument to bear against that. But the problem with Dees's criticism of evolutionary theory is that, although he rejects the Darwinists' answers to the questions of life, he has no answers himself.

And so here I sit beside my sleeping half-brother, who looks like me but then again not. The cuckoo's egg that my own father laid in my nest. Ever since Bo experienced the love of the girl-with-the-cap, he's no longer afraid at night. Love makes whole. But can love ever restore what's been broken between him and me? Will I ever be able to love him again the way I did all those years? And what about him? The only honest answer to those questions is: I don't know, by God – and not by Darwin either.

45

It was Bo's idea. It was profane, shocking and absurd, but I knew as soon as he suggested it that it would have to be carried out.

Four months had gone by since that insane day when he discovered that his father was his brother and his grandpa his father. From everything about him, you could tell that they had been the most difficult months of his life – nothing could change that, not even the postcards from the girl-with-the-cap. Throughout the summer, he looked as if it was still winter. He had bags under his eyes all the time, and he was even more taciturn than usual. Sometimes we would sit in the living room for hours without saying a word. Ellen let us go our way, the way only she could. She was there, even when she wasn't there. And she never got in our way, not even when she sat between us – in fact, especially not then.

For the first few weeks after that absurd discovery at my parents' house, I was so incredibly angry that at the end of each day every muscle in my body hurt. I often got up in the middle of the night and spent an hour under the shower, in the hope that I would then be able to sleep. Sometimes it helped. Usually it didn't. There was, however, one thing I did differently from what I had done in all the years before: I stopped drinking. On extremely bad days I pounded my head against the wall for minutes at a time. For days on end, I couldn't eat a bite.

Every day Ellen said, 'I love you.'

And sometimes I said, 'I love you too.'

And slowly the realization grew that although everything had changed, at the same time everything had stayed the same.

One Friday afternoon in August, Bo asked, 'How about us going fishing tomorrow?'

And of course I said yes.

He had just removed the hook from the first bream of the day and let it slide gently back into the water when he mentioned his idea.

'I want us to scatter Grandpa's ashes over Monika's grave. And then I want us to get on with life.'

The next day we stood at Monika's grave, Ellen, Bo and I. It was still early. The only other visitor was a song thrush, picking vigorously for worms on a freshly dug grave. Bo brought out the urn and unscrewed the lid. None of the rage and desperation of those days had gone out of the text on Monika's tombstone: 'Monika Paradies. Beautiful. Young. Mother. Dead.' I'd been ashamed of myself on occasion for not having come up with something more dignified. But now they suddenly seemed again to me to be the perfect words for what I knew about her. Once the love of my life. Now four words chiselled in granite.

Bo held the urn up as high as he could. Then he turned around and around. The fine dust blew across the graveyard in the summer breeze. A little white mountain formed at the foot of Monika's grave.

Acknowledgements

and

Word of Thanks

This book contains a number of direct quotations. The excerpts from the Gospel of Philip are based on the translation by the members of the Coptic Gnostic Library Project (*The Nag Hammadi Library in English*, E. J. Brill, Leiden, 1977), and on the Dutch translation by Jakob Slavenburg (*De verborgen leringen van Jezus*, Ankh-Hermes, Deventer, 1992). *Fulgor the Golden Eagle* was written by Cecilia Knowles. The various excerpts from the literature of biomedicine were taken from *Biochimica et biophysica acta, Molecular Cell Research* (Elsevier Science Publishers, Amsterdam, vol. 763, no. 2, September 1983). The figures on globe-theoretical decline were taken from *Pleidooi voor de platte aarde* (Plea for a Flat Earth) by Klaas Dijkstra (Boersma Enschede, publication date unknown).

During the writing of this book, I was assisted by the love, patience and professional wisdom of Tiziana Alings. Without her contribution, as critical as it was stimulating, this would never have become the book it is. These paltry words will never be enough to thank her.

Karel van Loon
Amsterdam, January 1999

Some great lines in bk 139
science facts re: sperm—true?
    theories built on shifting sand pg 152